When Fern up off the ground middle, it was a shock.

She was positioned on the horse in front of its rider, one muscular arm holding her fast against a rock-hard chest.

He smelled good.

That was the dizzying, nonsensical thought that crowded out all the other ones as she sat there, entirely trapped. He smelled like the forest. Like the sea. Like the wilderness itself.

Whoever this man was, he was a warrior.

She looked up at him and her heart leaped into her throat.

He looked like a Viking from the old world. He had long blond hair, and a full beard. His nose was straight and angular, his expression fierce.

This wasn't an agent of Ragnar, King of Asland.

This was the king himself.

His eyes caught hers and held.

Blue.

Shockingly blue.

And then it was all she could see, as her world narrowed and exhaustion rolled over her, claiming her consciousness.

Millie Adams is the very dramatic pseudonym of *New York Times* bestselling author Maisey Yates. Happiest surrounded by yarn, her family and the small woodland creatures she calls pets, she lives in a small house on the edge of the woods, which allows her to escape in the way she loves best—in the pages of a book. She loves intense alpha heroes and the women who dare to go toe-to-toe with them.

Books by Millie Adams

Harlequin Presents

The Forbidden Bride He Stole
Her Impossible Boss's Baby
Italian's Christmas Acquisition
His Highness's Diamond Decree
After-Hours Heir
Dragos's Broken Vows
Promoted to Boss's Wife
Heir of Scandal

The Diamond Club

Greek's Forbidden Temptation

Work Wives to Billionaires' Wives

Billionaire's Bride Bargain

Visit the Author Profile page
at Harlequin.com for more titles.

FROM CONVENT
TO QUEEN

MILLIE ADAMS

PRESENTS

MIX
Paper | Supporting responsible forestry
FSC® C021394
FSC www.fsc.org

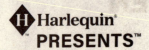

H Harlequin®
PRESENTS™

Recycling programs for this product may not exist in your area.

ISBN-13: 978-1-335-21362-4

From Convent to Queen

Harlequin Enterprises ULC
22 Adelaide St. West, 41st Floor
Toronto, Ontario M5H 4E3, Canada
www.Harlequin.com

HarperCollins Publishers
Macken House, 39/40 Mayor Street Upper,
Dublin 1, D01 C9W8, Ireland
www.HarperCollins.com

Printed in Lithuania

FROM CONVENT TO QUEEN

To Presents, which is always the place
for my imagination to run free.

CHAPTER ONE

THERE WERE BLUEBELLS as far as she could see. It was peaceful. So nothing. Nothing like she had ever experienced while growing up in the palace at Cape Blanco. Here, in the wilderness she knew peace. Here at the convent she finally felt like herself.

Fern.

Who felt so different than Fernanda Luisa Camila Esperanza Cortez, Princess of Cape Blanco, the small archipelago on the cusp of the Alboran Sea, crowded with her brothers and their aspirations of power.

They were all handsome and world-renowned for one thing or another. Juan—a great politician and heir apparent. Miguel—a financial genius, who was cold as ice. Julio—an actor, of all things. Rafa—a writer who seemed to delight in his own tortured mind. And Ricardo—who was perhaps the only brother who'd ever engaged her in conversation, but was a terrible rake, a model and a professional cad.

Fern was the youngest, and the only girl. Her lone claim to value of any kind was the marriage contract drawn up by her father with the presumed leader of

Asland. The island nation, populated by Vikings hundreds of years ago, had been ruled by a monarchy ever since—until the royal family had been overthrown in a military coup that had promised greater freedom but had ushered in authoritarian rule.

Fern's father had made a bargain with the president that Fern would marry his successor—who had been all but handpicked by the current president—when she was born. The union would ease trade between the countries and offer great military support.

Fern had been opposed. But it had also been a fact of her birth.

Like her green eyes, black hair and small stature.

Something she was born with. She might wish she was six feet tall, but she couldn't change her height. Just as she'd always wished she wasn't promised to be married off to a false president for the pursuit of yet more power.

But three years ago the authoritarian regime had fallen—a revolution led by the long-believed-deceased heir to the throne had upended everything, and restored balance and freedom to Asland.

King Ragnar was as formidable as he was dangerous—according to her father. And the agreement—should he choose to try and apply it under the present circumstances, could put them all in danger.

Which was when—at the age of eighteen—Fern had been sent off to the Isle of Skye to an isolated convent, where she felt like she had found herself for the first time.

Funny how she felt more...*her* in hiding than she ever had when living in the palace at Cape Blanco.

Or at the very least she felt connected to part of herself—her strength—that had never been allowed to blossom before. In the palace she'd learned diplomacy. Watching her brothers spar with one another had taught her well just what *not* to do.

What she had never been allowed to be was soft. It was far too dangerous. But here? Here she could embrace the quiet. The contemplation. The rhythms of nature. She had spent her life locked in quiet wars in the palace in Cape Blanco, and had never known who she was apart from that.

It had been an awful thing, her life in the palace. She'd had all those skills, and yet her word had never been respected. She was as smart and strong as any of her brothers, yet it didn't matter. She was forced into a mold for self-preservation, and then it wasn't even valued.

She despised men.

Men and their pursuit of power.

She had been steeped in it all her life. Her father and her five older brothers wanted nothing more than power. Her oldest brother—the heir to the throne—was as rigid and exacting as their father. And just as much of a liar.

Then there were the spares.

They were no better.

They spent their time in Europe, Africa, Australia, Asia, forging alliances and trying to jockey for power positions within their father's administration by greasing palms the world over.

When you were a small nation, diplomacy was of utmost importance. At least, that's what her father always said.

She didn't feel they excelled at true diplomacy. They were simply very opportunistic, and very practiced liars.

As for her, her entire function had been to become a wife. So she'd learned diplomacy of another kind— but while she'd been taking in her lessons she'd been learning other truths. She had learned that as long as she seemed biddable, as long as she kept her voice soft and expression sympathetic, she could often manipulate a situation better than her father or any of her brothers.

They didn't look for the strength inherent in women.

They didn't look for the steel in the softness.

They were a pack of misogynists.

Her mother had never been considered a full human. She was an accessory to her father, and if she was unhappy with it she never betrayed it to Fern.

Fern often tried to look through her mother's poise and impeccable manners to see if there was anything beneath them. To see if she was sad about the way she was sidelined, ignored and minimized.

Fern wondered if her mother had built a facade so thick and perfect that even she couldn't break out of it now.

All Fern had ever seen ahead for herself was more

of the same. She'd met the new president five years ago. A man in his forties with a charismatic demeanor that made Fern want to scream and run away and hide forever.

She'd been sixteen, facing down the prospect that in only two years she'd be marrying a man well old enough to be her father, but even worse—the same sort of man as her father.

She would never be free.

She would never have a life.

And all the things she'd learned—the ways she'd navigated her whole minefield-filled life—wouldn't matter because she would just be playing power games from behind the bars of a cage.

It had been a low moment.

Then Ragnar had taken the throne back in Asland and those plans had fallen apart.

She'd never been so relieved.

This man, whom she'd never met, had saved her.

At least, that was what she'd imagined. Until her father told her that Ragnar intended to marry her still—as the leader of the nation and the rightful beneficiary of the agreement.

She'd been sure her father would bundle her right off and send her into marriage with a total stranger—after all, he'd never cared what she wanted before.

But she'd tried to resist. To protest. She'd always thought it a useless thing to do, but faced with what felt like a certain demise or the futile defiance of her father, she'd decided to raise her voice.

To her surprise, he'd listened. She understood that

it was because he agreed—for some reason—with her concerns.

So now she was here. Hidden. Protected. Surrounded by other women, who found meaning in serving others and in sitting in silence. In serving the divine, not man.

It was a whole new way of being. One that Fern had never been exposed to before. At first she'd missed her phone—she had it with her but it barely worked. There was only wired internet available at the convent and only then in Mother Superior's study, and only used to communicate with the diocese and to receive time-sensitive information.

She had missed sleeping in at first too.

At the convent they arose at five to spend time with God. Though Fern had been given license to spend it in whatever type of meditative state she chose.

Eventually she stopped missing the fast pace of the internet and the constant relentless news cycle. Eventually she stopped seeking quick hits of shallow satisfaction from mindlessly browsing online. She started to look forward to the mornings. To the time alone with her thoughts.

She had friends now. She did chores. She took long walks. She read. She didn't perform, because the sisters had taught her that it didn't matter what a person pretended to be; it mattered who they were in their heart.

Here, she felt like her insides finally matched her outsides.

She didn't have to wear makeup or designer clothing to project her father's wealth and importance. She wore linen dresses and aprons. She had one simple pair of boots and a simple pair of flat shoes. She didn't add highlights to her hair or put ruthless straightening products on it anymore. Her curls were dark and wild.

She was wild too.

Perhaps part of the sweetness of the wild was knowing that it could be taken. If her father decided to come and fetch her.

If Ragnar found her.

Freedom was tenuous, and not truly hers, as ever.

If she thought about it too much it filled her with rage. But she was here. In the sun and the quiet and the glory, so she chose not to think of it.

She chose to be at peace, because she had otherwise never been permitted peace.

And in the three years she'd been here her disdain for her father had only grown. What had been a feeling—that he was wrong about most things—had become clear, fully formed thoughts now.

His manners weren't good. They were repulsive because they were lies.

He was rotten inside, and that was what mattered.

A person's heart was what counted, not their appearance.

Maybe he would forget about her here. She often fantasized about that. No one had been to see her in all the time she'd been in Scotland.

She was okay with that.

"Sister Fernanda." She turned at the sound of Mother Superior's voice behind her.

She wasn't a sister, but Mother Superior called her that to reinforce her place here, and the equality of all of them.

"Yes?" She squinted slightly, the sun shining in her face.

"Would you mind going and checking the bees and collecting some honey for supper?"

"Oh, I would love to."

Fern loved the bees. She'd found that she was very interested in all manner of farming practices, but cultivating honey was one of her favorite past times.

She went to the barn and gathered the beekeeping gear and a large jar from the shelf by the beekeeping suit, and walked across the expansive field toward the beehives.

At first, she'd been afraid of the bees. But she just hadn't understood them. She hadn't understood so many things.

She'd had perfect table manners but she hadn't been connected to the land, to the way that it fed humanity as long as humanity fed it back.

Now she knew.

She used her smoke to clear the bees away as she got into the hive and began to collect honeycomb and put it in the jar.

Then she walked back to the barn and took the beekeeper's suit off, holding the jar close to her chest as she walked back toward the convent.

Her stomach growled when she thought about the dinner they'd be able to have. They would have vegetables from the garden—potatoes, carrots and leeks. And there would likely be bread and butter, and now honey.

Though they were not entirely vegetarian at the convent, they ate very little meat, due both to the cost and to Mother Superior's general discomfort with taking life in any form, even if it was animal life.

Fern was so unaccustomed to that level of consideration and compassion. She'd been shocked by it at first.

Now she tried to cultivate it. To bring it into her own heart.

This deep caring about others.

This peace.

Silence had been all around, nothing but the wind through the flowers and grass, and then suddenly, the silence was broken by a rhythmic pounding.

She turned sharply behind her and saw a black horse with a large figure on the back of it, riding toward her at full speed.

She had never seen anything like this out here before. Had never seen one of the farmers from a neighboring property out riding like he was being chased by an enemy army.

She took a breath. And then began to run.

Without thinking. Without pausing.

Away from him or whatever might be after him. She felt like she'd fallen down into an alternate world—or maybe out of time, though that wasn't an uncommon feeling out here in the wild Highlands.

But this was uncommon.

This fear.

Everything here had always been peace and now she was running.

Why was she running?

And it hit her then, with each beat of her feet pounding the ground. She was running because she'd been sent here to hide.

Because if there was something to run from there was a high chance that the danger was there for her.

So she ran like she would die if she was caught, because perhaps she would be.

She ran like her freedom depended on it, because perhaps it did.

But she wasn't faster than a horse.

She could hear the hoofbeats getting closer and closer, and it confirmed that he was here for her. He was here for her.

Ragnar.

King Ragnar Gunnarson. Once deposed heir of Asland, now the king.

She didn't look back; it would only slow her down. So when she found herself being lifted up off the ground midstride it was a shock. She flailed and tried to escape the ironclad hold she found herself in, as she was positioned on the horse in front of its rider, one muscular arm holding her fast against a rock-hard chest.

He smelled good.

That was the dizzying, nonsensical thought that crowded out all the other ones as she sat there, entirely trapped. He smelled like the forest. Like the sea. Like the wilderness itself.

Whoever this man was, he was a warrior.

Her father and her brothers smelled of expensive colognes.

Not of the wild.

And then it was like whatever haze had fallen over her suddenly lifted. What was she doing, pondering the strength and scent of him and not trying to escape?

Without overthinking it, so that she didn't give her next move away, she arched backward and created space between herself and the rider, and then used that moment, that split second where he loosened his hold, to roll sideways off the horse.

She hit the ground hard, rolling to the side, and then stood up and began to run again. She no longer heard footsteps. She just had to get to the convent.

She just had to—

And then she was being lifted up again, this time, not onto the horse, but simply into the unseated rider's arms.

She looked up at him and her heart leaped into her throat.

He looked like a Viking from the old world. He had long blond hair, and a full beard. His nose was straight and angular, his expression fierce.

This wasn't an agent of Ragnar, King of Asland.

This was the king himself.

His eyes caught hers and held.

Blue.

Shockingly blue.

And then it was all she could see, as her world narrowed and fear and exhaustion rolled over her, claiming her consciousness.

CHAPTER TWO

SHE HAD FOUGHT him valiantly, and for that she had earned a small amount of his respect. But now she was unconscious and bruised besides for her foolish escape attempt, and that made Ragnar less inclined toward positive feelings for his wayward wife.

He hauled her back up onto the horse, adrenaline still coursing through his veins. He hadn't intended to turn this into a military operation but it certainly felt like a battle.

Why he'd thought it would be different, he couldn't say now.

All he knew was battle.

And this creature…

He held her firmly as he began to maneuver his horse around to head back to where they had come, to where his private plane would take them back to the palace in Asland.

He would have her examined by a doctor as well. He was certain she'd fainted from fear, but there was a small chance she'd hit her head when she'd fallen. Or rather thrown herself off the back of the horse.

Little fool.

It had been a long time since he'd held a woman. He pushed that thought, and any accompanying desire, aside. There was no time for that. There was a reason he hadn't indulged himself since taking over the throne. He had to stay sharp.

He felt the moment she woke up, her body no longer relaxed. She sat up against him, her body going rigid.

"Do not fling yourself down to the ground again," he warned, against her ear.

She turned just slightly, her expression fierce. "Let me go!"

"We have an agreement."

"I don't have an agreement with you."

"You do, signed by your father."

"I didn't sign it. It has nothing to do with me, except that my father decided my future without consulting me. That isn't an agreement with me. Just with the patriarchy."

"I will see the agreement honored."

"Then you're boring," she shot back.

Boring?

He had been called a great many things, but never boring.

"Yes. Because you're doing the exact thing that all men do. In the pursuit of power you will ignore everyone else."

"I am ignoring nothing, little one. I have a country to run and to stabilize. Your father promised you to the next ruler of my country, and that is now me."

"I don't want to go with you."

"I don't care."

If she was looking to find a man who might be moved to compassion by sorrow, or helplessness, then she was sadly looking in the wrong place.

All he had ever known was the brutality of survival. He didn't remember the details of his family. Oh, he had been old enough when the royal family had fallen that he should have some memories of them, of his life at the palace before. But they were gone. Erased by whatever trauma had come that day with the deposition of the king and queen.

With their execution.

He had read about it in documents, in news articles. The king and queen had both been slain in their seaside home, but he had no memory of that day at all, or of any of the days before.

It was his nanny who had helped him escape—so he had been told. Though she had passed him on to members of her own family and not stayed with him, and that was where things had gone wrong.

Everything crumbled. Nearly overnight. Any prosperity to be had in the country was gone. And he had been used for labor by the people who had taken him in.

At least there had been food and shelter. Though that had not lasted either.

Softness was not something he had experience with. She would not get it from him now.

"We are flying back to my country tonight."

"How did you find me?" she demanded, the haughty,

glittering green gaze that of a princess, however humble her clothing was.

"It was a mistake of your father to tell your brothers where you were. They're fools. Your father is not a fool, though he is a man who looks out for his own interests. I understand that he was afraid I would not be interested in guarding that which he valued. He made an alliance with my enemy, and I imagine he fears me for that reason. He should fear me. But with you in the palace, he should know that he is safe. But I will also expect an alliance in return."

"He isn't going to take kindly to you kidnapping me."

"But I didn't. Because he sold you to me. I will send him the bride price that is in the paperwork."

"A bride price?"

"Did you not know? It is not just eased trade and military alliances."

"Well, that means he decided that he didn't want the payment as much as he wanted to keep me safe."

"That is one way of looking at it, I suppose. The truth is, I think what he was afraid of is that I might seek to uncover some of the more nefarious things he engaged in with my predecessor."

"You can say whatever you want about my father, but Cape Blanco is not a dictatorship, and he did not commit human rights violations, not like the man who ruled your country."

"No," he said. "He didn't. You are correct about that. He was too smart to do it here. Too smart to do anything to his own people. But I'm willing to let bygones be bygones. For the strength of my nation."

If he could, he would see the destruction of every corrupt man. But unfortunately, corrupt men were the pillars of society. It made it difficult. What he had discovered when he had begun his mission for revolution, to reclaim the throne, was that he could not be a purist. There was no place in the world for a purist. Only for strength.

He could only do so much. He couldn't change the entire system. What he could do was save his own country.

And Princess Fernanda was part of that salvation whether she wanted to be or not.

"Are we riding your horse back to Asland?"

"Don't be ridiculous."

They had landed the plane in a covert area in a desolate place in the Highlands, with permission from the Scottish government. He had told them it was a matter of diplomacy, and no one had pressed. As long as he was leaving as quickly as he had come, no details were required.

The cargo area of the plane was open, and gripping Fernanda tightly, he rode the horse up the walkway and straight into the stable area in the cargo hold.

"Why the horse? You could have a fleet of sports cars down here."

"I could." He didn't offer her any explanation.

He didn't owe her one.

She was not so foolish as to think that her happiness, her desires, anything played into the way that the world ran. She was like him. In a fashion. She had grown up in a royal family. And even though he had grown up outside of one, the reality of being a king informed everything he did.

They might have been able to remove him from the palace. To remove him from the throne, but they had never been able to remove the responsibility he had to his country, to his people.

It was part of who he was. The very blood in his veins.

He'd had amnesia, still did. And yet he had always known who he was, with a deep certainty. There had been years when the true meaning of that had been lost to him, but he had never fully lost himself.

When he knew nothing, he knew he was the rightful king of Asland.

When he knew nothing, he knew that his father's blood called him to power.

"Will you tell me anything?" she asked.

"Do not bother me, or I will leave you down here with the horse."

"Well…"

She was clearly weighing her options. Testing him or complying. He didn't want to leave her down here, but he would. If she pushed.

He had no patience for hysterics.

He hadn't really gotten a good look at her yet. But as she stood there in the plain, glaring up at him, her green eyes glittering with rage, he finally got the measure of her. She was small. In height and in build, her figure neat and proportioned well. Her black hair went down to her waist, and was a wild snarl, all curls and now scattered through with pieces of the Highlands, since she had gone rolling in the dirt.

"Manage the horse," he said to three of his men who had come down the stairs. "I'm taking the princess up so that she may rest."

She didn't move when he did, so he gripped her arm up by the shoulder, his hand fitting entirely around it easily. He didn't have to hold her firmly to hold her strong. She moved in angry, halting steps behind him, going up the stairs and into the main seating area of the plane. He had brought a small contingent of his military with him, while leaving his highest-ranking generals behind.

There was a sense of real stability in his country now. Now that all of these freedoms had been restored, now that people were able to live again, there was a sense of calm, and he didn't worry about forces rising up against him. But he wouldn't take chances.

Not at this time.

He ushered her through the main quarters quickly, and took her back to his private office and bedroom area.

Her head whipped around toward the bed, her eyes going wide, as she looked up at him.

"Don't worry. I don't want your body. I want your bloodline."

"Wow. That is not reassuring at all. And seems to suggest you require my body eventually."

"We'll worry about that down the road. For now,

I have to concern myself with quickly and publicly marrying you before reaching out to your father."

"I have to agree to the marriage."

"You don't. The plane is about to take off, and then we will be in my country. I could stand in the center of the palace and declare us married and it would be so. You do not have to make vows to me. What I would like is a spectacle for all the world to see, so that there is no move your father can make that wouldn't receive so much public outcry that it wouldn't be worth it for him."

"But you require my obedience."

"You are with me now. You don't have the power. Let me explain this to you. We have an agreement. Your father is on the losing end of this. And I do not wish to make trouble for your country. But what I have done, what I have survived, is simply too high-stakes for me to leave any loose ends. This marriage was meant to happen. I need a wife. I need a queen. I can fight a war, but I do not know how to act on the throne, and I do not know how to…"

"Diplomacy?" she asked, her tone dry.

"Yes," he said. "That. I'm not a negotiator."

"I've noticed."

"You're not in any danger," he said.

"I'm not scared of you. If you care at all about public perception, then I don't think I have to worry about you hurting me. You should find another princess. I'm sure they would line up for the opportunity."

"But it's Cape Blanco that I want an alliance with. I need their trade agreements. Our country was increasingly isolated with that despotic dictator in charge. We were left devastated. And it is up to me to fix it. This is the only way."

"Surely it isn't the only way."

"It is the easiest way. And given that I have done everything up until now the absolute hardest way, a marital alliance seems like a good route to take."

"Marriage. Really. That's the only thing you can think of?"

"You say that as if I should have some sort of respect for the institution. As if it carries some kind of weight. I don't care about marriage. It means nothing to me. Family means nothing to me. You mean nothing to me. Nothing but a symbol. Get some rest."

And then he turned and left her.

It might seem cold to some. But he knew the truth. She would be better off without him near her.

It took about half of the plane ride for Fern to realize that she didn't have her phone. She didn't have any way of contacting anyone.

She had become so sporadic in her use of it that she hadn't been carrying it with her when she had been out today. She hadn't even touched it. But then the second thing that she realized was that she wasn't really in regular contact with anyone outside of the convent. She didn't have a network of people away from there. Of course, the sisters would do whatever they needed to to save her. She was confident in that. But she didn't know how they would do it.

There was nothing that she could do. She was physically outmatched. The man was more mountain than human. And on top of that, he had a whole team of men on board the plane.

She wasn't scared of him. Not physically. She knew exactly what King Ragnar had done when he had taken control back of his country. He'd dismantled the previous regime, sent the leaders to prison for the rest of their days.

He'd taken back the military—banishing all generals who opposed him.

He'd restored freedom that had been lost, abolished oppressive laws.

What he'd done had been for his people.

Which couldn't be said about the man that her father had intended to marry her off to.

Ragnar was still older than her. Though in his thirties, she suspected. She thought of the way he had looked at her with those cold, ice-blue eyes. He wasn't like the other president. He wasn't like the other man she had been promised to. But it didn't make her any more thrilled about being a spoil of war. Or whatever he had decided that she was.

A chip to be used against her father. To keep him in line. She suddenly felt very small. Impossibly so. Because this had been her fate for as long as she had understood it. She was nothing more than a bargaining chip. She was nothing more than a conduit for something else. And she wanted to be firm. She wanted to be inconsequential. Yet somehow larger in herself.

It was such a strange thing. She could be a political figure. She could be the queen of this country, but that had so much less meaning to her than waking up in the morning and tending a farm. Collecting eggs. Gathering honey.

She suddenly felt bereft about the honey that was lying in what was likely a broken jar, somewhere away from the convent. A waste of what they cultivated.

Emblematic of the last three years of her life.

It meant nothing.

No. It meant something. You learned about yourself. You know who you are.

She bolstered herself with that.

She knew who she was and what she wanted. She knew more about herself now than she ever had, and she knew more about the world. Funnily enough by being removed from it.

She was not in the same position that she would've been if she had been married off to a dictator at eighteen.

What a strange thing, that in many ways Ragnar's timing three years ago had saved her from something, and now he had come to collect.

She wasn't prepared to be a queen.

She didn't want to be trotted out all over the world, onstage, trussed up and living her life for public engagement.

And as the plane began to descend, she had a second thought.

She wasn't prepared to be a wife.

That thought made her face suddenly grow hot, made her stomach clamp tight.

She had intentionally never thought about that.

She had been promised to a man that she didn't want from her birth, so she didn't think about marriage and intimacy, and the fact that she was meant to carry a dictator's baby.

She didn't think about it because it was important. Because it couldn't be borne.

But now that she was here, on the edge of it, she couldn't release the thought.

He wanted to marry her immediately. Like he had said, he could stand in the center of the throne room and simply pronounce them married and they would be.

And then what? Would he want to consummate it like a medieval conqueror? Is that what it would take? To make sure that the marriage took. To make sure that she was trapped with him. Because that was what he would want. For her to be stuck with him. For her father not to want her back. And the truth was, him taking her virginity would go a long way in making her useless to her father. Her father wouldn't be able to simply farm her out to another world leader, would he? She would be damaged goods.

Men really were so boring.

She hated them. Every last one of them. And by the time the plane touched down, and Ragnar opened the door to the bedroom, she was nearly overflowing with hatred. Where was her peace? Where was all that peace that she had found in the convent? Where was the diplomacy that she had learned?

She was ready to fling herself right at him and attack, but the immense impact of him stopped her. It wasn't fear coursing through her veins. No. It was something else entirely.

He was big and broad, masculine in a way that nearly made it impossible to gaze upon him directly.

Perhaps it was simply because the convent was a female place. No men at all. Perhaps that added to the intensity of his impact. Of his...

Beauty.

The word sent a pang of fear through her.

No. She wasn't her mother.

She would not offer a brittle smile while she was broken into pieces. And she would not trade herself for the attentions of a man, simply because she found him beautiful.

"I'm not getting off this plane until we come to an agreement."

"I am perfectly capable of carrying you off the plane, little one."

"But not without the entire world seeing you man-handle me, *pendejo*, so I would assume that it's in your best interest for me to walk off here on my own two feet."

She glared up at him, resilience making her stand straight.

"What is it you wish to negotiate?"

"If I'm to be sentenced, then I want a term limit."

"Marriage is for life, my queen."

"Why?" The image of her mother, a beautiful, frozen emblem who lived in a house full of men who neither loved nor respected her, galvanized her now. "This is simply to cement trade agreements. To help you become the ruler that you want to appear to be. Why do you need me forever for that? You can find a new queen once you get rid of me. One to bear your children. To give you an heir. I don't want it."

"You don't want to be queen?"

"What I want is to be *free*."

"You want freedom from your father?"

"Yes. I will do whatever you ask of me as far as your image, as far as helping you with your present issues. I will not have a child. I will not share your bed. But I will get off this plane on my own, and I will look for all the world like a beaming bride. I am the only one who can give you the public-facing victory that you want. I am the only one that can give you your lavish, public wedding, because I have to look happy to be there. So you have to give me something."

"Two years," he said. "Or until the agreements feel eased. We may have to extend."

"Fine. That is fine with me. But you will not… I will not…"

Those blue eyes looked her up and down. "Do you think I'm about to fall on you like a lust-crazed animal?"

His words were so scathing, and she felt like she had been lit on fire.

"I know how men are. I grew up in a house filled with them. I know how little they respect women. I certainly know how little I've been respected."

"I didn't take you because you're a woman. I took you because you were useful to me. If the agreement was between me and the oldest son, then I would have taken him."

"Oh," she said, not certain of what to say to that.

"But alas, we live in a very traditional society, and you were the offering. But you are a worthy opponent. And I would prefer to have you as an ally." His eyes were sharp and clear as he looked at her. "You're very smart, aren't you?"

No man had ever said anything like that to her before. The nuns recognized that she was intelligent. But her father hadn't. Her brothers hadn't. If her mother had, she would never have said.

She had to resist the urge to feel pleased with her kidnapper.

"I could have been smart, or I could have been defeated growing up in the palace like I did. But my options were limited. It really was one or the other."

"You have a room prepared for you at the palace." She stared at him. "I was not going to force you into my bed."

She felt her face getting even hotter. "I didn't say that you were." Now she was reassuring her kidnapper? What was the matter with her? "I didn't accuse you of anything, but I wanted to make my stance clear."

"Are you a nun?"

"No. Though maybe I would like the chance to decide if I want to be one. Maybe I want the chance to decide if I want to be a pole dancer. Maybe I just want the chance. The choice."

"What a sweet, modern idea. Choices are rarely

actually available. And even when they are, they're generally an illusion."

"That's not true," she said.

"You challenge me?" he asked, clearly shocked.

She was used to men like him, though. It was true that in the space of only a few hours he'd shown her more respect than her father had in years, but that was more of a commentary on her father than on him.

But he didn't intimidate her—maybe he should. But what would he do? Hurt her and start a war? He wanted her for diplomacy and the truth was, he needed her.

In many ways, she'd probably never been safer.

It made her want to laugh except it wasn't funny.

"Yes. I do challenge you, because no one ever has, clearly, and they should. You men love to tell yourself you have no choice when in fact it simply means you take whatever it is you want. Saying there is no choice is an attempt at insulating yourself from argument. You didn't accidentally take the throne back over from an evil dictatorship. You had a choice, and you made your choice."

He laughed. Hard. Low. Rolling. It didn't make her feel amused, no. It chilled her. All the way down to her bones.

"Fernanda—" he used her name for the first time "—I bled for this. I fought my way up from nothing, for this. Perhaps, as you say, there was a choice, but as far as I'm concerned this was a mandate created in my very bones."

She gazed back up at him, and swallowed hard.

"That is spoken like a man. You believe that you're the only one in the world who can accomplish this, but you need to use me? I'm just an accessory to your goal, and as long as you say that there's no choice it justifies it?"

"You think that your happiness is more important than that of an entire country?"

"I have spent my entire life being told that I'm inconsequential. I cannot be nothing to my father, a thing to be manipulated and moved around at will, and yet essential to this."

"I never said you were inconsequential, and the truth is your father doesn't believe you are either. If he did, he never would have hidden you away at the convent. He would never have used you as a bargaining chip in the first place. This much you can know for certain. I have certainly never said you had no value. I would not have run you down on my horse if you didn't."

"Perhaps," she said, still making eye contact with him. "And if you had any sense of fairness you would have tried to capture me in a foot race so that we were evenly matched."

He nearly laughed; she was glad that he didn't. Because the sound of his voice, his laughter, was in no way pleasant. "Little one, I was not striving for fairness. I was intending to win. Rules and warfare are for other men. The stakes in this are too high for me to leave anything up to chance. For now, we have an agreement."

"And how am I supposed to know you'll honor it?"

He looked her up and down again, like she was a mere object. "You don't. You can only choose to take my word or not. But at the end of the day, any negotiating we have done is out of the goodness of my heart. You are my captive. And you will take what I give you."

Anger spiked in her blood, and she took a step forward, forcing herself to continue to look into those fathomless blue eyes. "You see how far you get if you have to drag me kicking and screaming off this plane. You see how well your plan works if your bride is a captive for all the world to see."

"You have to trust me," he said. "I have given you my word. I'm not your father. And I am not the man who held this position before me. I am the rightful king, and my only aim was to restore this country to its former glory, and then some. If you cannot trust in the goodness that may or may not lurk in my heart, trust in that. I do not care if it is you or any other woman who is by my side in my later years. I do not care if you are the one to give me an heir. All I care about is this. This moment. This agreement."

Whether she should or not, she believed that. Those callous words that might have wounded her if she cared even a little bit. But it was to her advantage that he didn't have any designs on her. To her advantage that he didn't care about her one way or the other. Specifically.

There had never been a silver lining to being a political pawn. There was now.

He stood tall, and held out his arm, and she looked

at him for a moment before realizing what she was intended to do. Then she took a step toward him, and placed her hand over his forearm, and allowed him to escort her from the room.

She kept her word. Part of him had expected that she would fight him, but instead she had done exactly as she had promised.

She had fire in her. It was a surprise. When he had discovered that the bride promised to the ruler of his country had been spirited off to a convent, he had imagined someone pious. Quiet. Prayerful, even. She was not a nun; that much was certain.

Not that he knew anything of the faithful. He had no use for fantasies. No ingrained connection to some spirit in the sky that was supposed to offer health, safety and blessing.

He had never experienced it.

No. When he had been alone in his life, he had been alone. There had been no comforting presence. No divine comfort to be had.

Still, he had thought that it might be a good thing to have a bride who had a more tempered personality.

She was not the one. It was no matter, however, because what he had said to her was true. He did not care how long they remained married. Once he felt secure in his position. Once the trade routes were well established, and they proved to be beneficial to everyone, once he had signed long-standing military treaties, he would have no use for her. He could trade her in for a new wife.

This one could be like another adviser. Not a wife in truth.

He looked down at her as he opened the door to the car that was waiting for them. Her eyes met his, and he felt the impact of her gaze like a freight train driving straight through him.

Apparently his body appreciated the challenge.

It was very like him.

If he wasn't fighting, he didn't know who he was. So in many ways, it wasn't a surprise that this woman who looked at him as if he was not great and terrifying, but was an obstacle to try to overcome, was appealing.

Most people found him frightening. For good reason.

He was barely more civilized than a wild animal. Than the wolves that had once famously roamed Asland. Women who were interested in him were often as hard as he was, experienced and jaded.

Princess Fernanda had a core of steel, but it was different.

She was not jaded.

She still believed that there was some measure of freedom out there for her to possess. Some great joy that she could find if only she were unfettered.

He knew that wasn't the case.

Responsibility would always pull you back, and if you owed yourself to no one and nothing, then it was simply a black hole of nothingness.

No purpose. No point.

And yet she was beautiful.

"Get in the car," he said. She obeyed, but she continued to look at him with those green eyes. He slammed the door shut, and got in on the other side.

"Shall we invite your family to the wedding, Fernanda?"

"Fern," she said.

"Excuse me?"

"I prefer to be called Fern. I don't like my full name. It makes me think of my father being angry with me. It makes me think of my time in the palace. At the convent, I was just Fern. And that's what I would like to be here."

"Isn't that a plant?" But as he said it, he thought that her eyes were rather that color. That cool green found in the depths of the forest. A plant that thrived even in darkness, even without the sun.

"Yes. And I have a greater connection to nature than I do to my family."

"Queen Fern," he said. "It does not have a particular ring to it."

"All the better that it won't be permanent."

"And you imagine when all this is over you will go off into a life of obscurity?"

"Yes," she said. "Why wouldn't I?"

"It is not feasible to expect that you would be queen of a nation and then simply slip off into the darkness."

"I suppose both of these things appeal to the rather erratic things I have been told all of my life. I am forgettable enough to slip into nothing. But important enough that I have to do this first. The paradoxical nature of being the youngest in a royal family. Of being the only daughter."

"I'm the only one," he said. "I wouldn't know."

Silence ruled as the car began to drive away from the airfield, up the winding road that would lead them to the castle on the craggy mountaintop. It overlooked the largest city in the nation. There was only one.

It was a small country, but with a rich history. Or at least, he would have considered it a rich history prior to the coup.

"Of course," she said, "I'm sorry. Your parents were killed."

"Yes," he said. "They were. A strange thing to have your personal tragedy in the history books."

She nodded. "I'm certain."

She looked…almost sorry for him and he did not care for it.

"But that is the problem with being in the position that you and I are in," he continued. "Our lives will never truly be personal. They belong to our countries."

"I can see why you feel that way. Because you're the heir. Because you're the only one left. It's nothing like that in my family. I have five brothers. In many ways, I am so unimportant because of my gender. And yet, in other ways… Had I been a sixth son I would truly have offered him nothing new. At least as a daughter I was able to offer the ability to enter into marriage agreements. He could sell my womb to the highest bidder. And did. But either way, I have never felt singular. Not to my country. I am only useful to my father's political ambitions. If I esteemed those ambitions then perhaps I would feel differently. But I don't. I don't care about what he wants."

"By all accounts Cape Blanco is a thriving country, particularly for the size that you are. Another Monte Carlo."

"My father is a capitalist. The fact that it is easiest for our country to be wealthy due to tourism is probably what keeps everything so stable. He wants it to be safe and attractive. Anything good that he does is a side effect of it being good for him." She paused for a moment. "That is perhaps uncharitable. He's not an evil dictator. But he did make a deal with one. And was not in any way hesitant to hand his daughter over to him."

"Did you have feelings for him?"

He felt that it was important to ask. If she harbored a connection to his enemy, then she could be a liability. It hadn't occurred to him until that moment, but what he was gathering from this entire conversation was that the marriage had been arranged in her infancy. Which meant she didn't know anything else.

Her face contorted in horror. "I absolutely had no feelings beyond contempt. I'm glad that he's rotting in prison getting everything that he deserves for being a despot."

"Then I find your father quite monstrous."

"Why? Clearly my free will doesn't matter to you. You don't even think I actually have it."

"I didn't say that. What I believe is that there are some things that bear so much weight your internal compass will continually point you back to them. What I believe is that eventually you realize your choices are not limitless, because the things that you believe in, the things that you value, will keep you on a path."

She looked out the window. "I don't even know what my path is supposed to be."

"Perhaps when this is finished you will find it." He found that he meant it. He found that maybe he even cared. Even if just the smallest bit. On the surface he had nothing in common with this woman, this princess who seemed to bemoan her life growing up in a palace. But in other ways, he did understand. Because he had been thrust into a life that did not belong to him, and he had been forced to claw his way back out.

It would be easy to write her off as being spoiled. Selfish.

But she hadn't had a chance to create her own fate. He supposed she was doing it now.

A valiant effort that he could only admire.

The car pulled up to the wrought iron gates that separated the palace from the rest of the world. Security was still extremely high, turning this place into a fortress. But they were such a new government, even if they were a continuation of the old. He took nothing for granted. For now, the people were happy. For now everything felt like a gain. But he knew how quickly the tide could turn. If there was a downturn in the economy, if something went wrong, then his rule would be blamed. There would come a time when what had happened in the past might not be at the forefront of their minds anymore. It had happened once. Only a fool would believe that it could never happen again, that he could be immune.

He turned to look at Fern, whose eyes were wide as she looked up at the imposing black palace.

"I've never seen anything like this," she said.

"Did you not come to the country to visit your intended?"

"No. I met him once. When I was sixteen. He was in his forties. It was at the palace in Cape Blanco. He made my skin crawl. I thank God that I never came here to visit him. Who knows what might've happened."

"Why *thank God*? If He truly wanted to help you He could have removed the problem altogether."

"He did," she said. "Eventually."

Her eyes met his and held, and her lips curved just slightly.

"Out of the frying pan, I'm afraid," he responded.

"But if I move quickly enough to the flames perhaps they won't scorch me."

He let out a hard breath, and when the car came to a stop, opened his door and rounded to her side. He did not allow anyone to open doors for him. He had not acclimated to any sort of royal protocol. It was clear, however, that the princess was accustomed to having the door opened for her. She had not made a move toward the car door one time since they had first approached the vehicle.

These were the sorts of things that betrayed her as royalty. He thought about what she had said. About the paradox of her existence. He could see it. Because there was wealth and high status in every line of her body. The way that she held her chin up high, the straight set of her shoulders. The imperious way that she spoke to him, even when she was at a clear disadvantage.

And yet she had no power.

She stepped out of the car, and he became suddenly very aware that she was not dressed in clothing fit for a princess. Thankfully there was no press awaiting his arrival today. They had no reason to. Another fledgling enterprise in this country—free press. For the last twenty-five years they had been nothing but a mouthpiece for the regime. He encouraged them to print the truth, and along with it their opinion. They were allowed to criticize him, and often did. They also watched many of his movements with great fascination.

When he did announce his engagement to Fern, and their swiftly impending marriage, it would create a firestorm. But thankfully, the fire hadn't started yet.

And when it did, perhaps it would be as Fern said. They would move through it quickly enough to not get scorched.

But in the meantime, she would need to be clothed in a way that befits the future queen.

He took her arm again, and led her to the grand front doors of the palace. It was made entirely of volcanic stone, the interior as dark as the exterior. There were sconces that illuminated the walls, but there was only so much light that could be introduced into such a dark antechamber.

Other parts of the palace had been made brighter with Sheetrock and texture, paint or wallpaper rather than this oppressive stone. But the entry and the throne room were much the same as they had been at the end of the Viking age.

"Medieval," she whispered.

"Yes. Fitting, given that it has been standing since the Middle Ages. Thoren the Bloody was the first ruler to take control of the nation, such as it was at the time."

"You're Vikings."

"Yes. Thoren and his company came here shortly after Iceland was taken away from the Irish monks. This land was barren, and was seen as a safe place for the Vikings to send their women, and to use as a base when they went on raids. The women of course came from all over, as you know the Vikings famously claimed brides wherever they went."

"You mean kidnapped and subjugated women."

"Most marriage was based on kidnapping and sub-jugation at the time."

She gave him a long, dry look. "Some still is."

He chuckled. He did find it amusing the way that she insisted on fighting him. "True. But you know, we famously have quite easy divorces."

"Do you?" she said, tilting her head. "Are you being serious?"

"Yes. And Viking women could divorce their husbands, as far back as the Middle Ages. They only had to declare it. This is still true. My country honors the old ways. At least we do again."

"And yet you seem to take a dim view on God."

"I would definitely be more inclined to say a prayer to Odin if I had the occasion to say one. But no."

"I imagine losing your family the way that you did…affected that."

"I thought you weren't a nun."

"I'm not."

"You seem awfully concerned about the state of my eternal soul."

"No. Just your…your peace, I suppose. I feel a great amount of peace in knowing that there is something bigger than me out there."

"If that's the case, why hasn't He fixed anything?"

"You're here, aren't you?"

"You can't convince me that I was meant to go through all of that."

They had paused in the entry, and he began to walk again, eager to get out of the conversation.

"How did you escape?"

"Why do you care?"

"If I'm going to help you, I would like to know you."

"You seem to be forgetting, you are my captive."

"No. You seem to be forgetting that we have a deal. And I don't want to be treated like a captive. But a partner." She stopped walking, and was looking at him with a mutinous expression.

He sighed heavily. "I don't remember. I don't remember anything about my life in the palace as a child. I don't remember how I escaped. I barely remember who I was. For years. I knew, but it meant nothing to me. It was like I was in a fog. It wasn't until I was fifteen or so that I decided I needed to make my way back here. That I needed to do something to fix what was broken. And that was when I began to make an army. As quietly as possible. Without tipping off the broader world that I was still alive."

"How did you do that?"

"Very carefully. Now, come to your room."

This time, she obeyed without pushing back. They walked up the spiral staircase, and into the more modern part of the palace. The hallway was well lit, with richly colored wallpaper that caught the light and didn't feel quite so oppressive. He preferred the darkness, personally.

The room that had been prepared for her was sumptuously outfitted. There was a canopy bed, a plush chaise, a bistro table and chairs so that she could take her breakfast in the morning. The bathroom had a glorious tub, and a large shower. His own room was completely Spartan. He didn't wish to get soft.

He still slept on a bedroll on the floor most nights.

It was hunger and a need for things to change that had gotten him here.

He never wanted to lose that hunger.

He was glad, too, that the seaside home his family had been killed in had been burned after the coup. It was why his own survival had escaped notice for so long.

It also meant he could never go back there.

Those memories would never find a foothold.

Her expression was dreamy, soft as she looked around the room. He imagined that she had been without such luxuries at the convent.

As if she had read his thoughts, she turned to him. "I was very happy at the convent. But I would be lying if I said I didn't miss having my own room."

"You shared a room?"

"Yes. With Sister Mary Celeste. Who was lovely, but did snore. And also the bed was a bit…sparse."

"Well, enjoy this. Because when you're off on your own replete with choices, how will you be paying for your life?"

It was perhaps a bit unkind to pose that question to her.

"I don't know. But I suppose I'll figure it out. I'll figure out what it is I want to do. Or maybe I will go back to the convent."

A woman of her beauty devoting herself to the church was a crime that his body rebelled against. He was intent on keeping his hands off of her. He had her for a limited time, and there was work to be done. There was no time for indulging in anything.

But still. He couldn't help but notice her beauty.

It didn't mean that he would act on that notice.

"Thankfully you have some time to consider it. In the meantime, the only thing you have to worry about is preparing to be my wife. I will be making announcements to the press tonight. We will marry on the balcony in front of all citizens who wish to attend. In the meantime I will have someone sent to make you look like a queen."

CHAPTER THREE

IN SPITE OF the fact that the bed was gloriously comfortable, she didn't sleep. She still didn't have a phone or a means of accessing the internet, so she had no idea what ripple effect Ragnar's announcement had in the rest of the world. Or indeed, with her family. Maybe they were drawing up a treaty. Maybe it had started a war. Why would anyone tell her? It wasn't like it was her life.

She had been stewing, also, on what he had said about her needing to support herself after the marriage ended.

She knew that. It was just that she had vague fantasies about waiting tables and living in a small cubby of an apartment while she figured all that out. She could go to Spain, Argentina, Mexico easily. Or to Canada, England or even Australia. Spain seemed the most familiar, potentially. Mexico was very far away. That held its own appeal.

It was difficult to know exactly what her dreams were. Because the biggest thing that had been hanging in front of her was her crushing lack of control over her life. If she had run away from home she would've been tracked down and brought back. There would have been no way for her to escape Cape Blanco. She wasn't anonymous. No one was going to help her get money or documentation that might help her escape. Again, part of the paradox of her existence.

She was in theory a person with power. Privilege.

And yet none of it was accessible to her.

Not when she wanted it. Not when she needed it.

It was why the convent had felt so revelatory.

She had been cared for, and there had been a structure, tasks, but there had been a lot of time for her to sit and think. But of course the things that she liked to do were the kinds of things everybody likes to do. She enjoyed reading. Sitting and drawing, even though she didn't have a talent for it.

Though really, if she could choose any sort of life, it might actually be on a farm. She could go from being a queen to being a farmer. She looked forward to telling Ragnar that was her plan. She hoped that it astonished and baffled him.

In fact she wanted nothing more.

Sparring with him was unlike anything she'd experienced before. There was something in it she couldn't articulate. Something—

The knock on the door interrupted her thoughts, and she was about to ask who it was when the doors swept open, and in came a servant pushing a cart that was laden with pastries and a pot of coffee. And behind that servant came two women, one holding a large kit, the other pushing a rack filled with brightly colored clothes.

She had slept in her dress last night, and she was feeling wrinkled this morning, and just looking at the sumptuous fabrics hanging on the rack made her feel a strange ache she couldn't recall feeling before. She hadn't missed dressing up, at least not consciously. In fact, she thought that she was happy to not have to go through the farce. The clothes were always chosen for her. It was never about her. Never about what she liked.

And of course this time it wouldn't be either.

"Good morning, Your Highness," one of the women said. "While you take your coffee and your breakfast we will begin to show you some options for today. Then we will bring in the wedding gowns."

"Oh?"

"Yes. Obviously you will need something for this morning, but then you will need to change for the wedding."

It wasn't entirely clear to her why she was expected to have more than one outfit. But she didn't complain—she couldn't. The first few dresses were lovely, pastel and made with sumptuous fabric. The kind of thing that would have been chosen for her to wear back home, but...

"You don't like them," the stylist said.

"They're beautiful," she replied.

"Yes. Of course they are. But they don't speak to you. If I may, I wonder if it would be better for you to look at some more saturated colors."

"Oh. Maybe."

She sat down in a chair. She wasn't sure why that happened, but then she realized that she had been ushered there by a handler who was so smooth he was orchestrating her movements without her even truly considering them. Her coffee was poured, pastries served. She began to eat, and as she did, the hairstylist began to arrange tools, and started evaluating her hair.

"I would like for it to stay curly," she said.

"Of course," the stylist said.

There was no *of course* about that at home. They said that her curls were unruly. That they didn't present a good picture of the crown. That they needed to be tamed, just like she did.

But if she was going to forge a different identity, it was going to start now. She could give Ragnar what he wanted. But she would give herself what she wanted as well.

Her hair was fussed with while she ate, and then she was presented with more dresses. And then, as if by magic, even more appeared.

The selections were vivid, and the winning dress was green, with long sleeves that were tight around her wrist and loose up to her shoulder. It fell softly down to her knees, the lovely, natural fibers in the fabric making it swirl delicately when she moved.

The sides of her hair were affixed upward, creating a slightly retro style that showcased her curls. And once they had settled on that, the wedding gowns came in.

A parade of glorious silks and satins. She chose the

simplest one. White and closely fitted to her body except for a train which flowed effortlessly behind her as she moved.

It was marked up to be fitted for this afternoon, and then she was put back into the green dress, and ushered out into the hall, and down the stairs.

Maybe she should feel something. Something more than she did. But marriage had never meant anything to her beyond this. An arrangement. Maybe in another life, with another set of circumstances, she would have been able to be romantic about it. But she never had been. She had only ever been able to be practical about the institution at best. And had dreaded it at worst.

She had never imagined marrying for love. But then, she had never imagined being able to marry for her own gain either, and buried somewhere in all of this was the potential for that.

She almost wanted to weep with relief. Reality hit, and hit hard. If she were being married to the president then her life would be over. She would be little more than his prisoner. And it would last for all of her life, a life that was determined by him. She would not have been choosing her own dresses; she was certain of that. Everything would be laid out for her. Chosen for her.

Even though she was being given choices within a set parameter, they were still choices.

This might be a tunnel, but it now had a light at the end of it.

The only other time she'd had light had been at the convent. Now she could take that experience, and she could make it into something even more expansive. Provided she got through all of this. She was guided down a long corridor, and then a large, black door swung open. There he was, sitting behind a desk. He looked up at her, those blue eyes burning bright in the relative darkness of the room. He had a weathered face. But it was no less beautiful for it. Each line spoke to worries he had carried for many, many years.

To the concerns that he had for his people. He was broad and muscular, and she thought then it was all the better for him to carry these burdens on his shoulders.

Do not romanticize him. He's another man using you for his own interests. Just because you can use him back doesn't make him benevolent.

It was a timely reminder. She looked over her shoulder, but there was no one there. All of the staff were gone. It was only her and Ragnar.

"Good morning," he said, lifting up the stack of papers on his desk and tapping them once, the gesture so clerical. So civilized that it seemed directly at odds with him.

He was dressed all in black. Not in a suit, but in a black sweater, and beneath the desk she could see black wool trousers and black shoes.

She hadn't noticed what he was wearing yesterday. Oddly, it had gotten lost in the kidnap of it all.

"Good morning. I assume that there is some public-facing event happening, or I wouldn't have been dressed like this."

"Correct. We are going to stream an announcement together about our upcoming marriage."

"What exactly are we going to say?"

"I'm going to address the nation. You are going to sit beside me."

"Am I meant to gaze up at you in adoration?"

"That is up to you."

"This is going to look like a political alliance, you realize that, right. I don't think people are going to find it overly romantic."

"I don't need my people to romanticize me. I need them to see me as someone strong and capable. Choosing you as a wife suggests that I am engaged in diplomacy."

"You also want me because I can teach you something about this life. My father isn't a good man. At least not on a personal level. But he is very good at making his people believe that he only ever has their best interests at heart. He's extremely charming. His manners are beyond reproach."

"Yes, as were my predecessor's. He would lie, and he would smile, and he would slither off into the ether to do vile things. I am exactly as I appear."

"Yes. But you might want to appear slightly more approachable. And you may want to let me speak."

She didn't really want to. It was one of her least favorite parts of royal life. Any of the times that she had been called upon to be part of the face of her country. Not because she didn't love her country—she felt deep affection for it, but she did not enjoy being in front of people. Still, the idea that he had, to present some kind of stony announcements to all the citizens of the country, with her sitting silently beside him like exactly what she was—a trophy representative of the revolution, and not a human being—was not going to do what he hoped.

"I think that we should say you and I have been working together on diplomacy. On easing things between our countries, healing divides. Even my father won't want to come and make trouble if I do that. I think that's been part of the problem. He hasn't known how to extricate himself from what until now had proven to be a very unpopular regime. Now that you're back, and you've had so much success, it's incredibly obvious that he would've been making a mistake marrying me off. I can fix that for him."

"And you want to do that?"

"No. I don't. But what I would like to do is make sure that my freedom is assured. By doing that, I need to bring my father on board with this arrangement. And I truly believe that we might be able to do that if I say the right things now. If I make it clear that my father supported your revolution, even if quietly."

"It is a lie."

"Of course it is," she said, moving up closer to his desk. "Of course it's a lie. But I was raised in this. This backstabbing, treacherous life. What I learned when I was taught manners and elocution was to look for the truth and meaning between the words. Manners hide all types of sins. They make it so a person can smile at your face while stabbing you in the side.

I did not make it this far in royal life without understanding that."

At least here that could matter. At least now she could use it. She felt a small measure of power now, in this moment. To finally be able to use the skills she'd honed and hidden in the palace. She was not the Fern she'd found at the convent now. But she was not the Fern she'd been in Cape Blanco either. It was like the two were coming together, and were stronger for it.

"A trade. We make your father look better than he is, and then he will not be able to interfere negatively with the marriage without damaging the reputation that you've created for him."

"Exactly. You and I have been working together on diplomacy."

She took a step closer, and for some reason her heart began to beat faster. "We began to develop feelings for each other. You are a man who has sworn to protect his country above all else."

"Won't that make our divorce more difficult?"

Her breath hitched. "Yes. It will. But I think it will also make everything seem like a better story. You don't want to present yourself as a man made of ice."

He shifted slightly, then stood up from where he was sitting. She had truly forgotten how large he was. She barely came up to the center of his broad chest. He looked like a relic from another time. One of his Viking ancestors brought forward to this moment. All he was missing was a broadsword.

"I do not mind my enemies thinking that I am made

of ice. You will be seen as a vulnerability—you realize that, don't you?"

"Do you have faith that you can protect this country?"

"Of course."

"Then you must have faith that you can protect
me. People would prefer if you had a vulnerability. It
makes you that much more human. You said yourself,
your ancestors initially brought their women here to
keep them safe."

"I believe that was more about possession than feelings."

"Why do you think that? Humans have always
found a way. Through all of history. We are a testament to that. We've found so many ways to survive.
Even when it seemed pointless. As for me, I found a
way to dream, even though my future seemed certain.
Wouldn't you rather know that a leader had a spark
of passion inside of him?"

He turned toward her, and even though there was
still space between their bodies she felt enveloped by
him. His presence was nearly overwhelming. Magnetic. He looked like a king. Like a man who was born
to sit on the throne. The truth was, he was the kind of
man that would instill confidence in anyone. Looking at him, it made her want to vow loyalty to him.
To hide underneath his protection. Very suddenly, the
idea of freedom felt frightening.

Don't falter now.

She took a sharp breath. "Don't be afraid to show
them your humanity. It is the lack of true human-

ity in the man who ruled before you that made him frightening. The ability to turn it on and off. You don't need to be charismatic. Be you. With a hint of a beating heart."

The truth was, he was charismatic. Just not in the way that many would define it. Perhaps *magnetic* was the better word.

"I will let you tell the story of us, then."

He gestured toward two chairs by the fireplace, where there was a stand in place for a camera.

"It is already hooked up to the broadcast channels, and to official online accounts. You and I are set to go on in one minute."

She didn't have time to protest, because he put his hand on her lower back and led her to the chair.

His hand was large, hot against her lower back, and she couldn't recall if she had ever had such close contact with a man as she had with him.

In fact, she had seen no man at all for the last three years, and she would have said that was a boon.

But suddenly she was very aware of him. The press of that palm against her back. And then she turned away from him and sat in the chair.

He sat beside her, and put his hand over the top of her arm, her hand.

His skin against hers electrified her.

And for the first time, she felt something that was truly like fear.

What was this?

But she didn't have time to question herself, because then the light on the camera turned on. He began to speak in Icelandic, and she did not know the language. She was suddenly very nervous, because they hadn't discussed what she was supposed to do.

They spoke English to one another, the common language between them, and that was going to have to be okay now. She imagined it was more likely that the people in this country would understand that, rather than her native Spanish.

She did her best to smile and to respond when she felt like it was appropriate.

"My fiancée will address you in English."

She felt a sweep of relief that he answered the question.

"Yes," she said, looking into the blank, dead eye of the camera. She was so aware of him touching her. And then he moved his thumb across her knuckles, and her heart leaped up high in her throat.

"Yes. I just wished to address all of you and say I am honored to be here. And to be part of this nation, and its new future. I have been working with the king for three years now, easing diplomatic ties between his country and mine. Over that time, he and I began to develop feelings for each other. So though this feels quick, I know, it is actually just a visible bloom on a seed that has been growing for a very long time."

"Our wedding will be this afternoon," he said, still speaking English. "We will wed on the large terrace at the front of the palace, and whoever wishes to attend may come and watch. This will usher in a new time. A new era. As we continue to work for the betterment of all people in our country. And with Queen Fern by my side I know that I am assured of this future."

The light on the camera went off, whoever was monitoring the broadcast clearly right on cue.

"Perfectly done."

"You don't believe in giving anyone much time to prepare."

"Nothing about you has suggested to me that you need extra time to prepare for anything."

She felt warmth, pleasure, spreading in her chest and she looked away. "Are you talking about the fact that I almost got away from you yesterday?"

"You didn't. But you tried. And then you skillfully renegotiated the terms of this arrangement. Somehow I knew that you would manage to do so again."

"That's a lot of confidence in a woman you only just met."

"When I was putting together my army—such as it was—to reclaim the country, I had to become an excellent judge of character. I couldn't afford to trust the wrong people. If the wrong word went into the wrong ear, the revolution would have been over before it began."

"So you're saying you're an excellent judge of character, and you have judged me to be excellent?"

"In a sense."

His hand was still resting on hers; she drew it back. And without thinking, brushed her fingers over his knuckles.

Those blue eyes met hers, and she felt something spark low inside of her.

Of all the things.

She had been immune to men all this time. Mainly because they had been adversaries to her.

She didn't respect them, didn't like them, so how could she ever want one?

Like marriage, romance had felt very much like it didn't fit into her life in a conventional way.

She wasn't certain that what she was feeling for him now was romance. No. It felt like something altogether more…earthy.

"The wedding will be in three hours," he said.

"Three hours?"

Suddenly, she imagined him pulling her into his arms and kissing her. Weddings had kisses. She felt very suddenly panicked about that.

"What am I supposed to expect with this wedding?"

"It will be quick."

"Okay. Anything else?"

"A traditional Aslandian wedding."

"I don't know what that is."

"Of course not. Because in these last twenty-five years my culture was nearly wiped out. Though I was living with villagers who still held to the old ways. And that's why I feel such a strong connection to those ways now. It is very much a warrior's wedding. There are vows, and then rather than a kiss, the husband cuts through his cloak and gives a piece of it to the wife. Binding both their hands with it to symbolize the union. But she has taken up his cause, and he has offered his protection."

It felt so grave. But it was a relief that she wasn't going to have to kiss him.

"You're not a very romantic people," she said. She said it to make herself feel better.

The space between his brows creased. "Do you not find that romantic? Perhaps it is because my life was marked by betrayal that I find the swearing of loyalty to be the deepest, most romantic concept there is."

"Do you?" Those blue eyes hit her hard. "I mean, do you feel that it's romantic?"

"No. I don't feel it. But I don't feel much of anything. Still, I recognize it for what it is."

"I guess that proves that I'm right, about the lack of romanticism here."

"I suppose that it does. But we will see just how much that is true by how many people come."

"Somehow I have a feeling that the crowd will turn out in force for their king that they thought long dead, especially now that they think he's found love."

He laughed, that cold, chilling laugh again. "It is best they don't know the truth. I might not have died that day, but most of me did. It will be a show. But as long as we put on a good one, I suppose it doesn't matter."

CHAPTER FOUR

He was dressed in a military uniform, one that denoted his high rank, and the accompanying cloak, which would be part of the ceremony. He found that he had underestimated his captive. She was extremely clever. Perhaps more clever when it came to these matters than he was. He would have to watch her closely. She had spoken of her father, said that he was manipulative.

It was clear that she understood the mechanics of manipulation.

He would have to keep special watch on her to ensure that she wasn't trying to do it to him.

Though what he had said to her was true. He did not have finer feelings. That made it very difficult for him to be manipulated. Though when he had touched her hand…

Yes. There were other ways to manipulate men. And he was no better than any other man when it came to matters of the flesh.

He had made a bargain with her. He would not take

her to bed. And at this point, it was for his own security as well as hers.

She was a very sharp knife in a drawer. A valuable thing, but if you reached around blindly, it could be used against you.

He walked out of his chamber, and down the stairs, toward where they would convene for the wedding, just as the door to her quarters opened. She came out, her hair styled elaborately, with white flowers placed in her dark curls, the wedding gown fitting closely against curves that had only been hinted at in the clothes she had worn so far.

She was so feminine and fragile. The kind of thing he would have to be careful holding in his hand. He had no gentleness in him. He could crush her far too easily.

That is part of her charm. Part of her ability to manipulate. Nothing is fragile about this woman, and you know it.

Yes. He did know that. Because she had fought him and fought him well when he had taken her captive. And when she had discovered that fighting him physically wouldn't work she had fought him with her wits. And now she had convinced him to create this story where they were in love. And he could see the easy merit in it. But he had to wonder if she was seeing something that he didn't.

She looked at him, and a delicate blush colored the top of her cheekbones.

Warmth cascaded through his bloodstream, and he chose not to question it, not to linger on it. Not linger on what she had been thinking or what he felt in response.

"Take my arm," he said.

He needed to become immune to her touch.

She was only a woman. It was only her hand. But he realized as the two of them began to walk toward the balcony that one thing she had done by turning this into a love story was cut him off from his ability to find release. He had been celibate for three years. The idea of being celibate for two more suddenly seemed unbearable.

He could make arrangements, he knew. He could have the women sign nondisclosure agreements. But she had made this very difficult for him.

"Of course, with the story that you have told, you've made it very difficult for either of us to take lovers."

Her fingers curled, her nails scratching him just slightly through the fabric of his military jacket. "Excuse me?"

"Now that you have painted it as a great love story, you have put us both in the position where any love affair we might have could be weaponized."

"I wasn't aware that you were considering having one."

"Two years of celibacy?"

"Ragnar, I have been in a convent for three years."

He might as well have been. Though he didn't wish to tell her that. Because it might give her the idea that she had more power to exploit.

"And before?"

"I was barely eighteen and living in a palace. You could put those pieces together yourself."

But they were then swept out onto the balcony, and he was prevented from following that down the logical road.

There was a sea of people down there, and the cheers when they came out were deafening. Even up there.

His country had turned out to see this. His people.

He felt suddenly overwhelmed. By a wall of something inside of him that was pushing against his chest. Creating pressure behind his eyes.

He had been cut off for all of his life. He had been alone. But these people, they had waited for him. They had needed him. This was why he had made it this far. He would not make a mistake now. He would not fail them.

He would manage this, all of it unerringly, for them. He would give them whatever they needed.

He took that feeling and pushed it down deep, added it to all of the dogged determination that lived inside of him.

This was the right thing.

So long as he remained in control.

The officiant came forward, an Orthodox priest who incorporated new and old ways. And he began to speak the vows for them to repeat. Ragnar realized that Fern would not understand.

"I give myself to you," he repeated in English. "For all of my life, and into the next. I give you my heart. My body. My breath. I give you my sword, to raise against your enemies, for they are now mine. In my home you are always safe. You are the most important battle I will ever fight."

He pulled his knife from its position on his thigh and grabbed the edge of his cloak, cutting the end off, and tearing a strip.

Her eyes were wide, the green more intense as she stared up at him. And he pressed his hand against hers, that strip of cloth held between their palms as he began to wind it around them.

The priest began to speak her vows. She looked at him, repeating the words as best she could, but clearly not knowing what they meant.

"Now I am bound to you," he translated. "To keep your hearth and home. To forsake the touch of any other, and their children for your name. My bloodline is now yours. Your home is now mine. I forsake all that I was, to become all that you need."

The color drained slightly from her face, and he tightened the cord, even more so cementing the bond.

"And what has been joined can never be torn asunder. Not with any sword wielded by the hands of men. For this bond extends beneath skin. To the soul. Unto heaven, and the underworld."

They turned and he held their arms up, so that the people below could see where they were bound. The cheer rolled through him, and then they turned and walked away, back into the palace.

Her hands were shaking, and she brought one over and began to fiercely undo where they were knotted.

"I… I need to get out of this. I needed to be untied."

"Stop," he said. "Steady yourself. Until we are alone."

He walked with her down the corridor, and into his study, where he closed the door firmly behind them with his free hand, and she continued to attack the knot like she was an ermine caught in a hunter's noose.

He flexed his forearm, and pulled, snapping the bonds. "There."

"Those vows are horrendously misogynistic," she said.

"How exactly?"

"I had to pledge my very blood to you, and you just have to fight for me."

"Unto death, Fern. I am obligated to lay down my life for you."

"You didn't have to pledge your cojones to me, however. I had to promise my womb." Color mounted high on her cheekbones. This time from embarrassment.

"The vows were for show."

"Maybe," she said. "But it feels like a very sacred thing to be taking lightly."

"How can it be both misogynistic and sacred?"

"I think you'll find that doesn't seem to be a conflict in most of humanity."

"You did well. You did exactly what was asked of you. And now we wait for your father to call."

"I'm surprised he hasn't already."

"He did. But I put him off until the last moment. And then expect…"

His phone rang. He went to the desk and picked it up. "King Octavio, it is good to hear from you."

"What have you done?"

"I've married your daughter. And now things will look different between our countries."

"Put her on the phone."

She tilted her chin up. "I have no problem speaking to him."

"English," he said as he handed her the phone.

She shot him a hard glare. "Hola, Papa. As you can see, I was taken from the convent. But I think that you will agree that the solution is a fine one."

"You cannot trust this man," he said.

"I don't trust him. But I do believe that we would be better served working with him rather than against him. And I did what I had to do to disconnect you from the previous dictator. You're welcome."

"He has not harmed you?"

The expression on her face shifted. "No. He has not. But thank you for asking."

He stole the phone from her then. "I have treated her better than anyone in your household ever did. I will be sending over my demands by the end of the week."

"You have the terms of the agreement," Octavio said in response.

"I will have the terms I lay out. You tried to run from me, Octavio. Men who run from me are always caught. Make no mistake."

He hung the phone up and tossed it down on his desk.

"He won't go against you," Fern said. "He's far too aware of his own need to preserve himself."

"You definitely made an impossible situation for him."

She laughed. "Well. Seeing as he spent the last twenty-one years putting me in impossible situations it feels almost poetic. I never would have thought that I could use any of these things to my own advantage. How nice to be proven wrong."

"A word of caution to you," he said, pausing for a moment and looking into those fathomless green eyes. "I will not be manipulated."

"Then continue to treat me like a partner and I won't need to do it."

He almost admired her. The way that she refused to cower. Refused to say that she wasn't trying to manipulate him, or that she never would.

She was intent on going toe to toe with him. It was difficult to object.

Because in his life, strength could only be admired. And he had to admire hers as well, even if he also had to be wary of it.

"You are not in a position to negotiate."

She smiled. "Neither are you. Now, we have married. What is it that you intend to do next?"

"I have new legislation to review."

"Do you have a parliament or anything like that?"

"No. There has been some talk of implementing one, but until then, I am mainly focusing on restoring functionality to the system."

"Is there anything that I can help with?"

He frowned. "I did not marry you for help with matters of state."

"In a fashion, you did. You said that you wanted me to help you with diplomacy."

"That's different. It is a woman's work."

He said it dismissively. Without thought. And when he looked back at her green eyes, she was giving him a deep glare. "What? Do you object to the characterization?"

"Yes. I do. Because I watched my mother be pushed into the background, disrespected, relegated to the shadows because her work was only a woman's work."

"You don't intend to stay here," he pointed out.

"No. I don't. How…was your parents' marriage? How did they balance things?"

And here was where that great yawning cavern existed. That place that stood empty. Meaningless. His past life before he had left the palace.

"I don't know," he said.

"You don't know it at all?"

"No. I've mentioned already, I don't remember how I escaped. I don't remember the day that the palace was taken. And I don't truly remember my life before."

"Did you…?" She moved closer to him, her scent intoxicating. She was like wildflowers and the forest. Something that he missed sometimes.

There had been few moments in his life when he had been a man without a mission. But when he had been simply a man, it had always been in the wilderness. He had given that up. He was a symbol now, not a person, and it was something he believed in. Felt keenly.

But it did not mean that sometimes the memory of his teenage years did not call to him. The lure of freedom...

She was a witch, perhaps. Her own designs on freedom infecting him. Informing him now, when he should not be thinking of that at all. He should be thinking about ways to continue to move his country forward.

She let out a breath. "We don't have to talk about it."

"It doesn't bother me. How can it? I don't recall it."

"Did you have amnesia? Did you have any idea who you were?"

"Yes. I did, but it only lived in the back of my mind. A very vague understanding. I knew my name, though they did not call me by my name. It was dangerous for anyone to know that I was alive. I understood that. I understood that I was the rightful king, but... I don't remember life here. I don't remember if I was close with my parents. It's all gone. Wiped away by whatever happened that day."

Her voice had grown hushed. There was softness now on her face that he had never seen directed at him before. "It must've been terrible."

"Happily, I don't know. Maybe it was. But it is not in my memory. I don't need it to be. That's what I've decided. It must be useless information. Everything that I have ever needed to know has been there. Every skill that I have ever needed to have has presented itself to me. This, I am certain, is no different. I misspoke. It is not because it is women's work that I need you to do diplomacy. It is because it is the one thing I don't understand."

"Well. That's better."

He didn't like admitting deficiency in any capacity. But a good leader also knew where his weaknesses were.

He would not hold his country back by being stubborn here.

"Well, that was my first piece of diplomacy accomplished—keeping my father from storming your shores—I will go away and ponder the rest."

"A good plan, my queen."

It seems a shame, to not be the one to remove her wedding dress.

The thought was so unexpected, the feeling that accompanied it so visceral, he had to brace his palms on the desk as she walked away from him.

He had never thought about marriage. Not beyond the potential for it to be useful politically. Not beyond the need to produce a child to carry on his bloodline.

He had not thought about it all those years, even when he was lonely in the woods. It meant very little to him.

He had always known that he wasn't part of any of those warm families in the village where he had grown up. That he was not part of the family in the household he was brought up in. He was different. Separate. Later it had become clear to him that it was a good thing he had always been held separate. Because his life was meant to be in service of others. It was meant to restore this nation. It was his responsibility. Born into his blood.

Marriage, family, love, none of that was part of it.

Still, right then, the place where they had been bound together by his cloak burned.

He had no explanation for that.

CHAPTER FIVE

SHE WAS HIGH on adrenaline. There was no other explanation. She felt like she had the energy of ten pikas trying to dry hay for their den before the winter came.

She was motivated, more than ever, to make use of these two years.

What she had learned from her time in the convent was that no time was wasted. Even when it felt like it was.

Her time at the convent had taught her more about herself than anything else in her life had. But it had been a quiet time. It had been a thoughtful time, where her own mind had been the teacher.

This was different. She had a job that she could do. She had a purpose.

He was right. She thought that she was going to go out into the world after this and just live a normal life. It was what she wanted. But she would need money. She would need education, a career.

Maybe she would start a farm. But she would need to understand what went into running it and keeping it going.

She could take advantage of this time. To learn. To gather what she needed. Because this was the beginning of something. Truly. She had help. She was not going to simply be an accessory to a man for the rest of her life. She was not going to rot away and lose herself the way that her mother had.

No.

That conversation with her father had proven to her that she had power. That she was smart.

She wasn't lesser.

She had won. Today, she had won.

"Excuse me," she said, when she saw the man that she had learned was Ragnar's right-hand adviser. Soren. "I need a computer. And an internet connection. I'm also going to need some idea of what the finances for the country are. And..."

"I will check with the king."

"Well, do that. But I'm not a prisoner."

"Are you not? I seem to recall that you were taken forcefully."

"But Ragnar and I have come to an agreement."

"I will see."

She gripped the front of her dress and swished back to her room.

It really was a lovely dress. She took it off, and went to her wardrobe, taking out a pair of camel-colored pants, and a loose-fitting top. By the time she was finished dressing there was a knock on her door.

"The king says you may have this."

She was presented with a laptop. Brand-new from the look of things.

She clutched it to her chest. "And?"

"He says he will send you information that might be relevant to you."

"How?"

"He established an email address for you."

And with that, Soren was gone.

And she set the computer on her desk and began to hunt through different webpages for information on Asland. Not just recent history, but the history of the past.

The history of what had happened at the palace on the day of the coup.

A coup that had resulted in horror for everyone.

The king and queen had been killed.

She knew that. Logically. But reading about it now that she knew Ragnar made her feel cold.

The young prince was eight years old. He was thought to have been killed along with his parents initially.

She squeezed her eyes shut as she realized that the implication of that was that there had been other victims who were children.

What an awful thing.

It made her feel a sense of deep anger at everyone involved. At her father. Who had formed an alliance with this new government rather than repudiating it. Who had done what was expedient to him at the time, rather than what was right.

There were no details about what had happened with Ragnar, because no one knew. His appearance on the scene had been a surprise to everyone the world over. But DNA results had proven that he was exactly who he said he was.

There was a dinging sound, and she opened up the email program. She smiled just slightly when she saw his name. In an email program. It seemed so weird and modern, civilized, when in practice that man was none of those things.

She clicked on the message.

You will find that the treasury is solvent. There is a budget in place for certain things. Why are you asking about this?

She tapped Reply.

Because, I'm thinking about what I do to accomplish diplomacy. And that might necessitate expenditures.

Another email came in quickly.

This is your budget:

The sum that he provided was more than generous. He had been right about the treasury being solvent.

Amazing, but she supposed that was what happened when a horrendous dictator hoarded everything for himself.

She could see by looking through all the information that a lot of the money had been returned to the people. The treasury was still healthy, and they were able to implement the sorts of programs necessary to keep a country running, but also there had been a real effort to lift the citizens out of the abject poverty they'd been forced into.

She sent him a new email.

I also want a list of countries you would be interested in strengthening ties with.

There was nothing in the body of the returned email. Only a document.

She tapped her chin as she read through it. And she began to formulate a plan. If he wanted to make a statement with their marriage, then they would make a statement.

A national paid holiday for all the citizens, with a celebratory atmosphere. And a party thrown at the palace.

For all of these world leaders that he wanted to strengthen ties with. Yes. She could do this.

She was confident in it.

She created a proposal, an outline for the events and how it would be executed. Of course, she would hire people who were more experienced than she was to oversee the details, but one thing she knew from her father was how to create a spectacle that would engage even the most jaded of guests.

She sent the proposal to Ragnar.

She was surprised when he didn't respond.

And when there was a deafening pounding on the door she nearly jumped out of her skin.

She scuttled away from the laptop, and opened

her door. There was Ragnar, standing there holding printed-out paper in his hand, glaring.

"What?"

"A party?"

"Not just any party, reception. For our marriage. To set our intention for how we intend to rule the country together."

"I do not do parties."

"You wanted me for this. You want me to teach you how to be with people. So you have to let me do what you've asked me to do."

"I don't have to do anything. I can throw you in the dungeon for the next two years—or forever if I like. That I have given you anything is a gift."

Her heart began to pound faster. "You are a beast. A flat-out monster, a feral animal who was raised by wolves. And if you want to be a king, a leader of men, then you have to start behaving like a man."

The tragic thing was, she felt like this was in line with men's behavior. She didn't give that gender very much credit at all. Her own life was a testament to how selfish they could be.

How difficult.

He let out a low growl and slammed her bedroom door shut as he walked inside. This was a huge space, and yet the way that he filled it was almost overwhelming.

Made it so that she couldn't breathe.

How could she be so angry at him and yet also…?

The truth was, she had spent her life exposed to men. But most of them had been her family. And the ones that weren't, were people like the vile dictator her father had been intent on forcing her to marry.

She had never been left alone in any sort of capacity with a man like Ragnar.

A man who was as compelling as he was terrifying.

A man who really might be closer to beast than human.

He was so large. So broad.

All of the men in her family had olive skin, black hair—like her own—and fine features. The kind that could easily put them on the cover of fashion magazines—and several of her brothers had been featured on such magazines. Ragnar was completely different.

He was rough-hewn, as if he had been carved from stone. His blond hair shaved at the sides, longer on the top, pushed back off of his face. His blue eyes were fierce, and his full beard added to his feral look. He didn't wear suits. Even today, he had been dressed in war regalia. And now he was back in the same all-black sweater and pants she had seen him in before.

There was nothing practiced or artful about him. In fact, he was frighteningly authentic and honest. He made her want to hide.

Not because of his broad shoulders and well-muscled arms, but because she was quite certain that he could see through her.

In a way that no one else ever had.

Maybe in a way she had never even seen herself. Not even after three years in a convent pondering her life, her feelings, her motives.

When he looked at her now, he made her throat go dry.

"You could keep me in a dungeon," she said, steeling up all her courage as she moved closer to him. "I understand that. But I don't think you will. You're a very smart man, Ragnar. Everything that I've seen of you so far suggests that. And you know that I'm no use to you if I'm a prisoner. If I'm a prisoner, then you could have taken any woman."

"That isn't true. I have now earned the allegiance of your father."

"You could have more."

Those words landed between them, and something flared in the depths of his icy gaze. Her heart leaped, her stomach going tight. And all at once it didn't feel like they were discussing diplomacy. Not a ball, not relations with Cape Blanco. All at once, it felt like something darker. Something more personal.

Something she truly had no experience with at all.

"Could I?" he asked, tilting his head to the side.

She curled her fingers into fists, her nails digging into her palms. A strange thrill shot through her core, and she had to fight the urge to press her thighs together. She didn't want him to see her react. She didn't want to betray the strange feelings that were rioting through her system, not at least until she could get a grasp on what they were.

"Yes," she said, swallowing hard. "In that I know how to manage all of this. I understand how to do this part. I learned from watching my father. And even though I don't respect him, even though I think he's kind of a terrible person, he is very good at making connections. So good that he even cozied up with an evil dictator. And he'll cozy up to you as well. He has no real morals where that is concerned. I do, though. I just also know…"

He lifted an eyebrow. "How to manipulate people?"

"I don't like to call it that. But I suppose it is. But isn't that actually what diplomacy is? You tweak everything just right until the other party is happy. In this case, we want them to see what you are offering. And why you're making things different. You've had a few years now to settle in, and now you've got married. So it's time to show everyone who you are now. And exactly where this country's going."

"It is a bit of a bait and switch, considering that you're a temporary addition."

"So you're going to have to outshine me," she said.

He chuckled. "Some have said that my personality is lacking."

"You said that you wanted help with that. Well, I can."

He moved to her desk and leaned back against it, and there was something nearly obscene about it, though she couldn't say why. Something about the way he held himself, about those muscular thighs, and how large and battered his hands were, gripping the edge of that desk.

She felt something that she couldn't even define inside of her. Something that was like instinct, as old as time. Something that was part of her, even if she didn't know how to define it.

She was innocent of men. In that way. But right then she felt like she knew. Exactly what she wanted from him. Exactly what she could do to him. And what she would want him to do to her.

Her breath caught. "I'm going to help you," she said.

"That remains to be seen."

He pushed off from the desk, and moved away from her, out toward the room. "We can meet tomorrow at noon."

"I will send you a detailed plan ahead of time."

When he left and closed the door behind him, a breath exited her body on a gust.

Now all she had to do was think of a detailed plan. And not about the way that her hands were shaking.

CHAPTER SIX

It HAD BEEN difficult to keep his hands off of her when he had been in her room. And the dark thoughts that had taken hold of him had almost made it more difficult, instead of easier.

Part of him wanted to push her. She wanted to use her body to manipulate him then...

Maybe he could show her.

Show her that if it became like that, he would have power over her too.

No.

He was not going to do that.

She was nothing more than another tool that he was using to bolster his country, and he would not allow her to become more than that. He got her itinerary, and didn't read it before he printed it off. But once he did read it, he found himself storming toward the study where she asked to meet him.

"Dancing?"

"People do love a dance," she said, standing up from the chair that she was sitting in. She was dressed in a white dress that fell just past her knees, the fabric diaphanous. Nearly see-through. It flowed when she moved, the bodice molded to her breasts. She looked like a virgin sacrifice. A goddess of old sent from Valhalla. The lust that gripped him was visceral. Beyond reason. It nearly blinded him.

And he felt his ancestors rising up inside of him. If he had a sword by his side he would've brandished it now and roared. Threatened to slay all enemies. Just for her.

"I don't," he said. "And I will not be doing it."

"I can dance with other men, but that will create conversation."

"If I don't dance, there doesn't need to be a dance."

"It's a party," she said. "There will be spectacular food, music and dancing. People enjoy it."

"It is opulence."

"People like opulence. And your people deserve a bit of opulence. Which is why I have suggested that a certain number of citizens should be invited to this."

"I'm not opposed." He was attempting to cool down the fire in his blood. "However, I am opposed to dancing."

"Why?"

He gritted his teeth. "I don't know how to do it."

"Is that all? I am an excellent dancer. Because of course I had to be, because I was being fashioned into a lovely, biddable puppet to best represent my country as the sort of feminine woman that my father wished me to be. I can teach you how to dance."

"Teach me?"

"Yes. Teach you. You wanted me to teach you

things, and I can. But you don't get to be picky about what it is I teach you. How can you know what you don't know?"

"This is ridiculous."

She picked up a remote control and pointed it at the corner of the room, and music began to play.

"Don't be silly."

She crossed the space and draped her hand over his shoulder.

On instinct, he put his hand on her waist. And he regretted it instantly. His fingertips burned. The dress was as thin as he had thought it was. He looked closely, he could see the shape of her pert breasts beneath that thin fabric.

It had been his opinion that pursuing sex would be a distraction as he had been reestablishing his country. He saw now that it had been a mistake to deprive himself. Because he was on edge. On edge in a way he certainly wouldn't be if it had been more recently that he had satisfied himself. Surely then he would not be half so taken in by the feel of her beneath his palm.

"Come on," she said. "I'm going to lead, just for the moment. I'm sure that you'll pick it up."

And then she was counting, as she gripped his hand in hers and began to guide him along. Her steps were decisive, perfectly in rhythm. He could hear the rhythm. He could feel it. He was used to the hoofbeats of his horse, the pounding of his heart, establishing the tempo.

He could understand dancing in that sense. But he

was distracted. Wholly and completely by the warmth of her body. By the shape of her.

The incendiary beauty when she looked into his eyes. All that green.

The song switched to something faster, and her steps picked up as well.

And soon, he had simply lost hold of himself. The time, the place, and why he had objected to the dance in the first place. There was nothing but this. But her. But him. There was no world outside these walls and it made him feel like he was something different than he had been all these years.

Perhaps a man and not simply a king.

The music changed again, this time going slow.

He found himself tightening his hold on her, his hand on her waist moving lower as he brought her body in closer to his. Her breasts touched his chest and he felt a shiver move through her body.

She looked up at him, and her cheeks were pink, her eyes sparkling.

She wanted him.

That much was clear. She was responding to his nearness, his touch.

As if you aren't being taken in by her.

For this moment, it didn't matter. As long as he knew what was happening. This was a dancing lesson and he was enjoying having a woman in his arms again. There would be no broader implications. Nothing that reached beyond that.

It was just a moment.

And in the moment it was all that was real.

"You lead," she whispered.

And then she was no longer guiding the steps. He took over, patterning his movements after hers. They moved together, the seamless rhythm shocking him as they hit each step in sync. Another man would be tempted to make a metaphor from it, but he didn't believe in romanticizing things.

He didn't believe in romance at all.

But the heat being generated between them now wasn't romance. What it was, though, was impossible to deny.

They were spinning around the room; he moved as if he were on air, and she was in the clouds with him. Perhaps that was close to romance as he would ever get.

Then he backed her up against the bookcase on the wall, without realizing he had gotten so close.

She gasped, and his body brushed hers. They were still then, only an inch of space between their mouths. He could claim her like this. Make her his wife in truth rather than just in name. He could lower his head and claim her mouth now. Taste her. Consume her.

She wanted him.

She was… She was enticing him.

He let out a hard breath and pushed away from her.

"I think you've proven your point. You are certainly an excellent teacher."

"You're an excellent student," she said, her voice sounding scratchy.

She seemed undone enough that he had to wonder

if it was as calculated as he had let himself believe for a moment.

But the truth was, it didn't matter what the truth was. The truth was, he was better off believing that she was a potential adversary, rather than simply believing she was a woman caught up in the moment as he was a man wrapped up in it as well.

"What else do we need to go over?"

"Probably manners."

She moved away from him. He had to hold back a growl.

"Are my manners lacking?"

"They could be a little bit more polished."

"Perhaps you simply don't understand my culture."

"I believe that you have a distinct culture here, don't mistake me. I just also believe that you personally have been out of society for enough time that you probably need a little bit of help. It isn't just about your culture now, it's about global relations anyway."

"I probably had excellent manners at one time. Pity that it's lost along with everything else."

She turned toward the bookcase and touched a blue spine, then looked at him. "You really don't remember anything?"

"No. Nothing."

He didn't feel inclined to elaborate. So he wouldn't.

"Did people have a lot of questions for you when you…when you appeared?"

"No," he said. "I've barely talked to anyone who isn't part of my…"

"Your personal military attaché?"

"That's one way of putting it."

"People will have questions for you. They're going to want to hear your story. Eventually, all of the people in your country are going to want to hear your story. And why wouldn't they? I was reading up on the history of your country. You're part of the history of this country. And people are going to want to know everything."

"They don't need to know everything."

"Well, maybe you can figure out something to tell them. About how you lived, about how you saved them. You're so difficult sometimes."

"I wasn't aware that entertainment was in the job description."

"But you know that it is. Because people want to feel like they know and understand their leaders. I'm sorry if it seems silly to you, but it is true. One of the reasons my father is able to get away with being so slimy behind the scenes is that he is so charismatic when he's on stage. He's a man who understands that he has an audience. And that the audience has to be played too. Understandably, your country has been in survival mode. And so things have been different for you. But somehow, all those years ago, your relatively happy, harmonious country was overthrown. And the horrendous dictator that led the charge was supported by your people at first. People blame their problems on the government. That's just the way it is. Even if the government didn't cause them. Their anger and their desperation allowed them to walk right into authoritarianism."

"Are you implying that charisma on my part might prevent that from happening again, or rather that a monosyllabic answer might send us tumbling back into the Dark Ages?"

"Yes. Yes, I am saying that. People want to feel a connection from you. I know that you care. I know that you lived, to spite everyone. Despite everything. That you survived for these people. They should know it too. They should understand how much you do care."

"Do you really think that people want to hear about the days and weeks and months that we spent camping out in the wilderness, trying to evade detection? Do you think they want to know that I lived as a farmhand? What kind of confidence will that instill in them?"

"Plenty. You are truly a man of the people. You fought for them. You have lived for them so strongly up until this point. And I think that you should talk about it. This is what you have me for. Whether you realize it or not. It isn't just about royal protocol. You need somebody to make you human."

"I don't want to be human. Humans are weak. They are weak and they are susceptible to cold, to fear and to hunger. Exhaustion and hopelessness. A symbol cannot experience any of those things. I would rather that they saw me as a warrior."

"Does it have less to do with how people want to see you and more to do with what you want? Because you don't want to feel those things anymore?"

"If you think that you can trick me into some sort

of sharing moment, you will find yourself disap-
pointed."

"If you don't want to share with me, then you don't
have to."

"You sound like a kindergarten teacher."

"You're acting a little bit like a kindergartner."

Her gaze went steely. There was something about
that challenge that ignited a flame inside of Ragnar.
What he wanted to do was close the distance between
them and push her up against the bookcase. He wanted
to bring his mouth down on hers. She was being in-
solent. A brat.

One thing he could not recall was the last time a
woman—anyone—had challenged him. Not outside
of a life-or-death situation, at least. And so it created
this bonfire of adrenaline inside of him that left him
breathless and trembling with the intensity of it, yet
also gave him no immediate relief.

Because what he truly wanted, he could not have.

"I will go to your ball. And I will dance with you,"
he said, moving toward her, his heart raging now. He
felt dangerously close to being out of control, and that
was not something he had experienced in a very long
time. He didn't like how raw it made him feel. How
precarious. How much it reminded him of...

Of something he didn't want to know about.

"But I will not be manipulated into sharing. I will
not be manipulated—"

"And why are you so convinced that I am manipulative? What is it that makes you think I'm trying
to trick you?"

"I don't know," he said. "Except that I have watched you. I have watched you play your father, and I am not convinced that you aren't playing me."

"And what makes you feel that you would be vulnerable to that?"

He growled and moved toward her, trapping her between his arms, pressed against the bookcase. He glared down at her. "I told you. I'm not sharing my feelings."

She smelled like the field that he had found her in. Like spring, fresh and new. Like the kind of tender hope he himself could not recall ever experiencing. She was devastating to him, and it made him want to beat his chest. It made him want to start a war.

It made him…

She reached up and touched his face, and he drew back. It broke the spell.

"Do not," he said.

"Ragnar," she said, her voice steady. "What are you afraid of?"

He laughed. "I'm not afraid of anything. Are you? But perhaps you should be."

"I'm not impressed by dark muttering. I'm not impressed by the way that you deflect constantly. You've turned it back around to me, when we were talking about you."

"I did not choose to talk about me. You did."

"Maybe I'm not thinking clearly. But it seems to me that there is something," she said gently, slowly. He didn't like it.

"There is nothing," he said.

And he felt like he needed to claim control of the situation. Felt like he had no choice. "The only thing it's bringing up, is this."

And then he closed the distance between them, and claimed her mouth with his.

CHAPTER SEVEN

SHE HAD PUSHED him into this. She couldn't lie to herself. She had wanted it. She couldn't lie to herself about that either.

But she wasn't prepared for it. He claimed her mouth like the conqueror he was.

It was an absolute undeniable conquest. His mouth was hot and firm, forceful. She parted her lips for him, and he claimed yet more ground. Sliding his tongue against hers. The guttural moan that rattled through him sending a sharp shock of pleasure down between her legs.

This was desire. All at once, she understood. She had so deliberately held herself back from it. And who wouldn't? When your whole life already belonged to a man you didn't want, why would you ever let yourself think about sex, about desire or about what being married would mean? She had deliberately shut that part of herself down. And now, here it was, awake, alive with the pleasure that he was creating in her body.

This was the kind of thing that she had feared for all of these years.

And here it was. It wasn't scary. It was glorious. The kiss was hot and slick and created a cascade of sensations that weren't confined only to her mouth. She could feel him everywhere. It was like a brand that heated her entire body. That scorched her from the inside out.

His hands were large, and he moved them down and grabbed hold of her hips as he continued to kiss her, deeper and harder.

Like everything else about him, there was nothing soft or tender.

But she would rather have that. The honesty of this moment. Free of…manipulation.

He was so very afraid of manipulation.

Just as that thought passed through her head, he pulled away from her. And she could breathe again. Except she didn't want oxygen; she wanted him.

And suddenly she was furious. That he had accused her of manipulating him. When he had all this power. All this experience. When she had been left with no choice but to use the cleverness at her disposal in order to turn the situation into anything other than captivity. Lifelong captivity for her.

Why was it wrong for her to try to get whatever she could out of this? Why was it wrong? It made no sense.

His worries were those of a man. Knowing that emotions that he hadn't cared for or honed could be used against him. That his baser appetites could be used against him. While her worries were those of a woman. Knowing that she could be physically forced into whatever a man deemed her lot in life. Whatever he decided.

Because he had been so angry. But as long as it had been his idea, he got to kiss her.

She pulled away as much as she could with the bookcase still at her back. "Who is using manipulation now?"

"That was not manipulation."

"Oh no. I forgot. Forcing your way is an asset. Trying to have some diplomacy is apparently duplicitous."

"I didn't say that."

"Here's a question I have for you. Why shouldn't I use what I have in my arsenal? Why should I lay down to be a conquest for you? In any capacity. I am a human being. And I have hopes and dreams. You can laugh at them all you want. You can say that I have no choices, but I want to see for myself, and I deserve that. I don't deserve to be passed around by men. As they decide what they think is right for my life. I deserve to decide what is right for my life. And if you find that selfish while you remain in total control of everything, then perhaps you need to ask yourself why you don't think a woman deserves the same rights that you do."

She slipped away from him, and he grabbed her arm. "It has nothing to do with you being a woman. And everything to do with the fact that you were what I needed to accomplish my goal."

"Even better. It isn't personal. So it isn't women that don't matter to you. It's everyone."

"I have sacrificed my whole life to liberate my people. I care for the greater good. Not for the individual."

"I don't think you care for anyone or anything. I think you're driven. Driven to win. Driven to dominate. Everything. Including me. You thought you were going to a convent to pluck a helpless woman out of her life and force her into yours. You call manipulation me having a voice. Me pushing back. Only because I'm not what you expected. Only because you expect everyone and everything to fall in line for you. I will help you with your ball. I will do what I said. Beyond that… I will please myself."

She turned away from him, and she stormed out of the study, down the hall and toward her chambers. She was done. Done with all these men. With their designs on her life. She was not a chess piece. Why was it that when men could do something it was a strategy, while she was…manipulative?

She stormed into her room and shut the door behind her loudly. If he could hear, if everyone in the palace could hear, that was fine with her.

What was the point of being a queen if she had to keep her voice down, had to close the door quietly? What was the point of being a queen if she still had no control over anything?

This life…

This was her life for the next two years. Dealing with this man.

She was trembling still. From the kiss.

He was…

Outrageous.

Yes. He was outrageous.

He had given her her first kiss. And it was still echoing inside of her.

Need was warring with anger. And she found that even more outrageous.

How could she want him when he made her so angry? How could she want him when she also wanted to strangle him?

Two years of this. At minimum. That was depending on whether or not he found that things were secure enough by that time.

He had all the control. That bastard. No. She had some control. He wouldn't be worried about manipulation if he didn't think that he could fall prey to it. Like she had said to him directly.

She definitely had power over him. He wanted her.

That was a part of herself that she had ignored. And certainly not something she had ever sought to use as a weapon.

She still didn't want to use it solely as a weapon.

But...

Two years.

She wanted it to mean something. She wanted to count for something. She was learning things. About herself. She was learning by planning this and...

She was innocent. Physically. Maybe there was something that she could learn here about that. About men.

She had been promised to marry a man twice her age. More than twice her age. And then Ragnar had stolen her, and his initial intent had been to make her his wife in truth.

Men had played games with her, and with her sexuality for her entire life.

The idea of having the choice for how she would express it, when she might claim it, made her feel powerful.

Maybe it shouldn't. No, she knew that it shouldn't. Because it should be something that was innate. Something she expected. It never had been.

She had never been able to count on such a luxury.

So maybe now she would. Maybe now, she would take what she wanted.

She could seduce him.

It didn't matter that she didn't have any experience. She had gotten a glimpse of her own power in that library. Had truly tasted it as she had tasted the desire on his tongue.

More to the point, she wanted him. Whether she liked him or not.

Even as the thought filtered through her mind, she let out a long, slow breath.

She did like him. Unfortunately. If she didn't like him, then him calling her manipulative wouldn't have hurt her feelings.

But maybe it was a good thing he had called her that.

It had forced her to take a look at herself. At her whole life.

She didn't feel any guilt for what she had done to give herself just a little bit of agency.

She refused to.

He was just…

Traumatized.

She really didn't want to feel sympathy for him. But it was impossible not to.

He had been traumatized. Absolutely and completely. The little bit that he had told her…

But he couldn't remember anything. Not about his parents, not about his life here in the palace.

He couldn't remember anything.

It must haunt him.

Perhaps it wasn't as haunting as remembering. That did make her feel sympathy for him, even though she didn't especially want to.

He was human. It would be easy to let herself forget that. To tell herself that his humanity didn't matter in the face of all of the ways in which he was difficult. But the truth was, he wasn't entirely different from her.

He had experienced a life that was laid out before him; he had been taken as a child, and treated like an object. His life had not been of his own making.

Maybe she wasn't feeling benevolent; that was pushing it a little bit far. But maybe they could both have something nice in these two years.

Maybe if she asked he could do something for him.

Not just to set herself free. But to free him too.

And something about that made her feel powerful in ways she hadn't expected.

He had managed to avoid her other than the few times he had been pulled into her orbit during the planning of the event. She had asked him to consult on the menu. That had been interesting.

Truth be told, he hadn't expanded his palate much beyond meat and potatoes. And meat had been a luxury for many years. Not always guaranteed.

But she was asking him to try seafood and pastries, hors d'oeuvres and tiny cakes that looked like they would be at home in a bakery window.

In fact, looking at the tray had given him a visceral memory of walking by a bakery in a small town very soon after the coup.

He had pushed it aside, and hadn't allowed himself to make any connections between the past and the food in front of him.

But now it was the night before the ball, and he could no longer outrun her.

"There are three suits for you to choose from," she said.

"I had thought that I would wear a military uniform."

"I appreciate your commitment," she said. "But I think that in the spirit of the evening you should go with a suit."

As if this had been timed, a tailor came through the doors of the study, with a rack full of suits.

Well. She wanted to do this, so she could stay.

He took his shirt off, and turned to the rack of suits. "What is the difference between these?"

He looked back at Fern, who was staring, eyes wide.

"If you do not wish to be involved," he said.

"I'm going to be involved," she responded.

He undid the buckle on his belt, worked it through the loops, and then cast it onto the floor. Then he took his pants off, which left him standing there in his black undergarments. And he could sense her eyes on him.

He looked at her again; her face was bright red, but she wasn't backing down, and certainly wasn't making a move to leave.

Well. It turned out he was not above a little manipulation himself. Not that he was trying to get her to do anything. It was only that he was proving to himself that she wanted him. And that it wasn't simply a tactic on her part. The look on her face made it clear.

"There are three different styles," the tailor said. "A more traditional tuxedo, a suit and then a slightly more modern choice."

"Traditional," he said.

"That is shocking," Fern said.

"Is that a commentary on how predictable you find me, my queen?"

"Perhaps," she said. "But you should know that I'm not shy about making commentary. I said exactly what I meant."

"Of this I am aware."

"I think you should do the suit," she said. "I think it will feel more natural to you. More black. Less cummerbund."

He lifted a brow. "I'm not even sure what cummerbund is."

The tailor took a strip of shiny fabric off the rack.

"It's this."

"No," he said, the rejection easy.

"I thought I might have guessed correctly."

Which was how he found himself being dressed, and his wife watching all the while.

His wife. She wasn't truly his wife.

She was…a complication.

He had been turning over their conversation in the library for days now.

The way that she had spoken about him not liking to be manipulated… Who did?

She spoke to him as if he had some sort of hidden trauma—well, he did. He knew well that he did.

His brain protected him from whatever it was that had befallen him the day of the coup, and beyond that, it had protected him by not allowing him to remember the happier times of his family. Which would have only been painful. He could only miss the idea of them. But not them.

He didn't bemoan the missing memories.

But she made him wonder… No. There would be no wondering.

The suit was fitted expertly to his body, then removed from him. And before he could dress again, the tailor left to see to his work, and left him, wearing nothing, standing there with Fern.

"Obviously, I couldn't act as if your body was a shock to me. We're meant to be married." She turned away from him.

"Is that why you were staring so intently?"

"No. I was staring intently because you have a nice body."

She looked over her shoulder. "You must know that's true."

"I've never thought about it one way or the other."

"Surely you must know that somehow your lovers respond to it."

"Are you interested in having a dialogue about my previous lovers?"

"Perhaps."

"Whatever game you're playing, I don't like it."

"Must everything be a game?"

"I fear that everything must be."

"And if it wasn't, I suppose then it would be very serious, and would therefore have much further reaching implications."

"Perhaps."

He put his pants back on, buckled the belt. She was still determinedly turned away.

"And what are you wearing to this event?"

"That's going to be a surprise."

"A surprise? Why?"

He wanted to know. And yet at the same time he didn't want her to know that it felt significant to him. But he was allowing himself to imagine her in a glorious gown.

He hadn't seen her in anything like that since the wedding.

She had been...a vision.

Resplendent.

He had wanted her.

Utterly.

He still did.

This was the trouble with living with a woman. With her being his wife, even in a place the size of the palace. He couldn't truly escape her.

"I didn't know any of my previous lovers," he said. "It was always opportune moments. Towns that we would be passing through."

"Ah. I see. So casual sex is your thing."

"I wouldn't say that. I would say that much like I would try a different pub when we passed through towns, looking for whatever meal we might find, getting something to satisfy my hunger, I would treat sex the same way. It is an appetite, nothing more. There is no need to feel shame about it. There is no need to turn it into something more than it is."

"Spoken like a man."

"Why do you think that's masculine of me?"

"Because you have the physical power. Even with this life that you didn't choose, nobody sold your body away. By promising me to a stranger, my father promised my virginity to a man that I didn't want. By kidnapping me and intending to take me as your wife, you laid a claim on it too. But you don't think about being forced into bed, do you? So, of course, to you it feels simple. Of course to you it feels like something that shouldn't carry weight, or shame. But for me, it can't be that way."

Her words were sobering in a way he hadn't anticipated. "But I have not forced you into anything," he said, the incendiary kiss burning between them.

"No," she said. "You haven't. But I didn't know that. Not when I ran from you. You think that my wanting choices is silly. You think that my having dreams is silly."

"You said this to me once before."

"And you didn't understand. I can understand why that feels shallow to you. Why can't you understand for me that it feels like everything?"

"I don't have practice trying to understand other people."

"Did you even have friends growing up?"

"No. I was a servant, for all intents and purposes."

She turned around and looked at him, her gaze landing at the center of his chest, and then quickly moving to his eyes. "A servant who was meant to be king?"

"It wasn't so bad as that. It was lonely. But then I had a lot of time to decide who I was going to be."

"Did you have a mentor? Somebody who…came alongside you and told you that you were the chosen one?"

"No. I decided to be the chosen one. I decided that nobody was going to fix the mess. And that it was my blood that made it my responsibility."

"You never thought about running away and leaving this place?"

"No. Because these are my people. I owe them my best attempt. Even if it isn't perfect."

He had never shared any of this with anyone before. It was strange. To talk about something so personal.

He had been a symbol of revolution. And he had

found people who agreed with him. When he wanted them to fight alongside of him, and form a coalition to oust the government, he had no longer been lonely, but what they had spoken of was not personal. They had spoken of ideals. They had spoken of government. Of war. They had been prepared to die if need be. But then they had managed to get the military onto their side. And it hadn't been necessary.

They had taken everything down from the inside; by the time he had walked into the throne room, it had been reclaimed.

A bloodless revolution, even though he had been prepared for violence.

This woman… She challenged him. Danced with him. Got him to talk to her.

It was such a strange thing.

And he found that the more he spoke to her, the more he wanted to speak to her.

It was like one of those little cakes. He had tried one, and it only made him want another.

He was studied in self-denial. Much less so in the craving of things.

"And what about you? You grew up entirely in a palace. And yet you were not treated like royalty."

"No," she said. "I told you I have five brothers. And my father could only use me one way.

"My mother was just… I don't know why she married him. It was just because she had aspirations to be queen. If it was political, if her hand was forced the way that my father intended to force mine… I don't know, and I don't know that I ever will. Because I don't know how to talk to her. It's like she's withdrawn from her own life. All she cares about is fashion and manicures. I like those things too, but I also like to speak about other things. I judged her harshly for a very long time. But now I wonder if that's simply how she survives it. But I couldn't do it. I couldn't hollow myself out to be a vehicle for a man's plans."

"You were going to do what he wanted," he said.

"I didn't especially have a choice. You would think that I would've missed the opulence of the palace when I went to the convent. I think my father thought that I would. I think he found it somewhat amusing. Like it would be lowering for me to be sent there, like I would maybe learn a lesson, and be more grateful. But I wept in relief when he left me on the Isle of Skye."

Her eyes filled with tears even speaking of it.

"All I wanted was to be left to my own devices there. And I did find the divine. I did find a connection to myself that I didn't know I could have. I found thoughts that I'd never had before. And strength, much more strength. I thought a few times about running away when I was in the palace, but I really didn't know how to survive away from my family. Or what it would look like. But one of the reasons I ran from you so easily was that by then I knew what independence felt like. I didn't want to go back."

"You don't like being royalty?" Guilt lanced him. It was so unfamiliar he almost had a difficult time identifying it.

"No. I don't. I find it to be…" She stopped speaking. "I don't actually know what it is to be royal. For me it has always meant existing to do the bidding of someone else. Not even for the good of my people. Maybe I would feel differently if I was the one in charge. But for me, it has meant living a life of gilded subjugation."

"Your father's foolish for not respecting your mind. I understand why you're angry at me, but I fear that you are clever and insightful."

"You fear it? *Well*." There was some satisfaction in that word.

"A brilliant mind is a fearsome thing."

"You were so angry at me that night."

"I'm not accustomed to…" He didn't even know what to call it. Whatever this was.

"Friendship?"

Friendship. He turned the idea over in his mind, and felt that it fit the situation uncomfortably.

And yet, it was possibly closer than many other things. He had shared things with her that he had otherwise never shared with anyone.

He felt compassion for her. Even sadness when she shared some of her life in Cape Blanco.

"Friendship," he said again.

"Yes. Or maybe we're moving toward something like it. Is that so absurd?"

"Not absurd," he said. "Just…unexpected."

"If you let me, if you stop resisting, it really would help you."

"I still don't wish to tell my life story to strangers in a ballroom."

"You don't have to. But it would perhaps be good to have an easy version of events that you can share."

"Ah yes. For my place in the history books."

"You don't care about that, do you?"

"No. All I wanted was to survive for this moment. For this task."

"And do you know what to do now that you have survived?"

The question was pointed. And he still didn't have a shirt on. He wanted to move closer to her, and put her hand right at the center of his chest, where her eyes kept dipping. But he supposed that wouldn't be the act of a friend.

Part of him rebelled against that word. He was a warrior, a conqueror, and he should behave in that way, not like this.

And yet her words, the revelations that she had given him about her life, the way she had been treated, the lack of choice, made him…

Care.

He was used to caring about causes, not about people.

But perhaps it was the next step. What came after survival.

Living, in some capacity.

"We would be having cake at the ball?"

Cake seemed easier than whatever was happening now.

"Yes," she said, scrunching her nose up. "There will be. I noticed that you liked it."

"Oh. That is… Thank you."

CHAPTER EIGHT

HE HAD THANKED HER. He had thanked her for the cake.

She had been thinking about that ever since, along with the vision of his body, covered only by those tight black boxer briefs that he'd been wearing.

She was extremely distracted. Even as she got her hair and makeup done, and was zipped into the gold gown that she had chosen for tonight.

She had been thinking about him far too much.

But it was okay, actually. Because she had made a decision about tonight.

Tonight was important. And she was going to sparkle, build connections and keep him on track for the whole of the celebration, and then she was going to seduce him.

Because she wanted him.

Because she felt they both deserved…

Were they friends?

It was the word that she had come up with when they had spoken.

She wasn't sure she'd ever had friends either. The nuns were the closest thing. And they had been tasked with taking care of her, and also had very little in common with her in some ways.

It had been a contemplative life. But sometimes it had been fun, and sometimes they'd had deep conversation.

Yes. In the three years that she had been there it had definitely been something like friendship.

So maybe this could be too. Maybe they didn't have to be at odds.

Maybe she could learn physical things from him, so that when she went out into the real world, none of it would be shocking. Perhaps it would be easier. She would know how to deal with men. How to be normal.

Preferable to going out into the world as a twenty-one-year-old virgin, she supposed.

She clung to the idea of a life opened up. Of a life where she made her own choices.

And in the meantime, where she could make her present situation all the more pleasant.

Where she could learn about herself.

She had done that thoughtfully, internally on the Isle of Skye.

Maybe it was time to do it physically.

Her makeup had been done expertly, in that way where it took quite a few products and skill to accomplish a natural look.

And her hair had been left curly and wild as she had come to prefer it.

She felt like herself. And that was interesting. To feel at home in her skin in this sort of dress, when that had never been true back in Cape Blanco.

The plan for them was that they would arrive thirty minutes after the guests. Wherein they would be presented to those in attendance. Fashionably late.

Her stomach fluttered. Not because of the entrance they were going to make soon, but because soon she was going to see Ragnar.

It was amazing what that did to her. How it made her feel. How in this short span of time he had gotten beneath her skin. He had found the power to affect her body.

The first time she had seen him, riding on that horse, the thunderous hoofbeats sending terror streaking through her, her reaction to him had been pure adrenaline.

But now? It was still adrenaline, she supposed. But it was something deep. Something more. Something nice.

It was…attraction. Need. This luxurious, wonderful feeling that she had been prepared to never, ever feel, in defiance of the life that her father had laid out for her.

As a way to maintain control.

And now she didn't want that. She didn't need it. Not in that way.

Feeling it was control of a kind. It was a type of power.

As if a door inside of herself had been opened up for the first time, as if she could suddenly feel everything. And it wasn't all contained inside of her. Wasn't a private, secret thing that she could never share with another person. She wanted to share it with him. To make him feel what she did.

Which was maybe a bit of a lofty goal for a woman who had until recently never kissed a man.

But she was hungry. Maybe some people would think that this was Stockholm syndrome. But she didn't think that she was very susceptible.

If so, she might have had different feelings about her father. She certainly didn't.

Time had never made her look more fondly upon him regarding the things he was trying to manipulate her into.

It had never made her warm to the idea of marrying a stranger.

Ragnar was different. Yes, he had taken her captive, but when she said what she wanted he listened. He might initially be dismissive. He didn't know how to deal with people.

He might sometimes be insulting, but he didn't have any friends.

It had nothing to do with respect for her, and she actually believed that now. Now that she had gotten to know him just a little bit better.

Now that you've seen him in his underwear and you've decided that he's so hot you don't want to keep your hands to yourself anymore?

Even if that was the case, she wasn't going to question it. It was an experience that she was hungry for.

She wanted to indulge her appetites. The way that she had seen him indulge himself with those hors d'oeuvres that she had prepared for the party tonight.

Neither of them had had very many nice things in their lives.

Even when he spoke about his past lovers he didn't make it sound fun. He made it sound ruthlessly efficient, like everything else he did. As matter-of-fact as eating a bowl of stew, which was not the way that she wanted to imagine sex.

Maybe she would find that she was the one who was wrong about the whole thing.

Maybe.

But her entire life had been marked by being both sheltered and unprotected. Sheltered from anything that she might want, from the kinds of normal mistakes and experiences that other people were able to have. While also being set up to marry a man who wouldn't treat her well. A man she didn't want.

Any protection that she had received had been about what her father wanted, and not actually about her.

So if she made a mistake now, if she slept with Ragnar, and got hurt, if it made things difficult when it was time for her to leave, that was a consequence that she was willing to accept. Because it was her consequence. Because it was her right to make those mistakes.

He wasn't pressuring her. It was her decision.

She felt his presence when he entered the room, and she turned sharply, just as he stepped fully through the doorway of the antechamber to the ballroom. That black suit that he had tried on the other day now fit his muscular body to perfection.

That broad chest, narrow waist and the thoroughly muscular thighs were still visible, his appearance only just on the correct side of civilized.

His blond hair was slicked back off of his forehead, shaved tightly at the sides. His beard expertly trimmed. His blue eyes were as arresting as they had been the first time she'd seen him. And it was interesting to feel the subtle shift in her response to him. Now when her heartbeat picked up it wasn't fight-or-flight.

It was desire.

She recognized that. Purely. Absolutely.

His eyes skimmed over her curves, and she felt that look like a brand. He was difficult to read. Nearly emotionless. But the heat in his blue gaze didn't lie. The intensity. Especially now that she recognized the difference inside of her, she could see it in his gaze.

It wasn't simply the triumph of a conqueror closing in on his conquest. It was desire. Just like her own. A mirror into the deepest parts of herself, all fathomless blue.

"You know the goddess Freya?"

She shook her head.

"No."

"She is the goddess of love, beauty. Sex. But also war and gold."

"That seems a strange combination of things."

"Not really. For what do we fight wars over except love, sex and gold?"

She had never thought about that before. Gold, yes. Greed. That was the biggest reason she could think of for war. But throughout time, and in small ways, every day she supposed people did wage battle for love and sex. Need, erotic need, was something she was currently fighting a battle inside of herself about.

"Freya rules Fólkvangr. A heavenly field where many soldiers who die in battle go."

"I thought that in Norse mythology they went to Valhalla?"

"Some do. But there is a different path. Some in my culture think that it's soldiers who are loved that go to Freya. Because she saves a space for their wives."

"Oh."

"You look like her. Freya."

She laughed. "That can't be. I'm hardly a Scandinavian beauty."

"Your lack of blond hair doesn't make you less a beauty. Freya herself is brave and bold. Clever. As a goddess must be. There is also sadness in her. I would say that you are definitely Freya. All that gold."

It was the most deeply beautiful thing anyone had ever said to her. And she felt seen in a way that she hadn't expected to be seen by him.

She would've said that they were different. Entirely. But they weren't.

They were two people who had been deeply isolated in different ways throughout their lives.

And the only time in his life when he'd had a family he couldn't even remember.

He was a warrior, yes, but he must've spent a significant amount of time in his own mind. Thinking. Making a declaration like that proved it to her.

"I didn't think you believed in the divine," she commented.

"I never have."

Then he reached his arm out and she took hold of it. He didn't say that he did now. Or that he was changing his way of thinking, and yet it felt like he had paid her a glorious compliment all the same.

Maybe this was just her shifting and twisting the moment to make it into something undeniable. So that when she kissed him after the ball tonight, she could justify it.

I don't have to justify anything.

No. She decided that she didn't. She decided that she didn't have to have any reason other than the fact that she wanted it.

Because she was entitled to that.

After everything, surely she was entitled to that.

They walked through the double doors of the ballroom, and the scene below took Fern's breath away. The room was full, and decorated gloriously. There were fresh flowers strung across all the surfaces, bright pinks and purples that were set off beautifully by the black walls and gold trimmings.

The light, natural beauty was unexpected in the heavy, medieval surroundings.

And even more wonderfully, the room was filled with people. Some she recognized from events at the palace in Cape Blanco, and abroad. Others she suspected were citizens from this country.

And all heads turned to look at them as they walked out to the top step.

She curtsied, and Ragnar gave a deep bow as they were introduced.

"His Royal Highness, King Ragnar. And his queen, Fernanda."

She could forgive the use of her full name. Here it seemed right.

She was firm with Ragnar, and that was good enough.

The sense of warmth that radiated inside of her when she thought of that surprised her.

It surprised her that it mattered.

That there was something between the two of them that she didn't share with anyone else.

His hand felt warm on her arm as the two of them began to descend the stairs.

She looked at him; his face was stern. Unapproachable, even though she had a feeling he didn't mean to be. She smiled. Doing her best to look easy for the two of them.

Yes, she was doing her best.

Because she actually cared. This wasn't just about blending in. It wasn't just about being the perfect accessory. She was actually trying to help him. She believed in this.

She believed in him.

This country was beautiful. Though she hadn't seen as much of it as she would like to yet. She had fully been realizing how much she had in common with Ragnar, but she also had something in common with the people of this country.

They'd had their choices taken away from them.

Their lives had been stolen from them. Their freedom had been stolen from them.

She felt a burning desire to change that. To bring back their sense of identity. To restore their dreams.

If she could do it by smiling now, then she would.

Ragnar bypassed several members of the ruling class and nobility from other countries, and she felt like she needed to offer an apologetic smile as they made their way past. But then she realized. He was moving toward his citizens. His people.

The woman that he approached looked startled, and then she began to bow.

He shook his head. "We will not stand on royal protocol," he said. "We are family. United in our desire to change things for this country. For the better." He stuck his hand out, and the woman took it. He shook it. His expression was grave, but it was real. Authentic. And she felt a surge of pride inside of her.

"I'm Fern," she said. Because she decided that she would give their people that name as well. They went around and introduced themselves to every single citizen of Asland, just like that. There were tears. At one point a woman hugged Fern.

They were so hungry for joy. For a sense that someone cared about them. About how they were doing, and about their futures. The futures of their children.

An older woman clasped Fern's hands in hers and looked up at her with shining eyes. "Queen Fernanda. When you have children it will be such a blessing."

A pang of guilt shot through her. Because she was planning to leave. She was forging these alliances, these relationships, and then she intended to leave. She had this idea of getting on with her life, and she was overwhelmed with the deep realization that this was their life.

They weren't just passing through. And she had to give this all the care that she would if she planned to stay forever.

Children.

If Ragnar had heard any of the exchange, nothing about his expression indicated it. She could see that his people appreciated his strength. That they responded to his demeanor. He seemed sincere because he wasn't putting on a show. Because he was sincere.

It made her chest feel sore.

She had this idea of the way things had to be, and it was based on the actions of someone she didn't even respect.

Ragnar had to be free to be the king that he was.

Still, she had been right to have this.

She did most of the talking when they interacted with diplomats and royals, while Ragnar ate an entire plate of small cakes.

It was perhaps the most delightful thing she had ever seen. Tiny, pastel cakes in his large hands.

He was enjoying them; she could see that, even if his expression remained stubbornly neutral throughout.

The band began to play, and the large dance floor was cleared. "We have to dance first," she said.

He nodded slowly, and then he held his hand out to her.

She curtsied, and then placed her hand in his. He wrapped his fingers around hers, completely engulfing them.

And then he pulled her out to the center of the floor, his arm tight around her waist, his other hand holding hers like she was anchoring him.

"You remember," she whispered.

Of course, when they had practiced dancing, things had not been so easy between them. And what she remembered wasn't just the dancing. His resistance. His angry kiss.

Her heart began to beat as he took the first step in time with the music. As she moved with him.

As he swept her over the dance floor and she kept imagining his mouth on hers, her back pressed against the bookcase. His hard, hot body right on hers.

His hands. Those large hands on her hips.

And she could see the memory reflected in his own gaze. In the blue depths, fire and ice and all that he was.

He was such a complicated man.

A puzzle to be solved. And maybe she would make that the mission of the next two years as well.

To untangle all of the aspects of him. To find the man beneath the warrior. The man beneath all of his pain.

She wondered about his missing memories. Would he ever get them back? Was it more of a blessing if he didn't?

She wondered about all of that while memories of the kiss echoed persistently in her brain.

While he held her close, in time to the music, beneath the keen gaze of their audience.

And finally, halfway through the song, they were joined by the rest of the attendees at the ball. Still, even surrounded by all those people, it felt like they might be the only two in the world.

A dangerous feeling. When they were here to serve. When they were here to be of use to the people of this country. To forge alliances. They weren't the only two people.

She had to remember that.

But tonight would be for the two of them. On that she had decided.

They danced through several songs, and then exhausted themselves making another circuit of the room. Until they had spoken to everyone. She could feel Ragnar losing strength. And it made her think again about his life. About all the things that he had done. And about how few of those things included these kinds of arduous social situations.

Of course it was exhausting. The man would probably rather be on a battlefield.

As soon as the clock struck midnight, it was their cue to leave. And they were officially excused as they had come in.

Once they were out in the antechamber, in the silence, away from everyone, she turned to him. "I don't wish to go back to my room tonight."

"You do not?"

"No. I intend to go back to yours."

CHAPTER NINE

RAGNAR HAD NOT anticipated this.

He felt like his skull was about to implode. He had
not spoken to so many people in all of his life, let
alone in the compressed space of a few hours. And
yet there was more. Touching her for hours had left
him on edge. For a man who had spent so much of his
life in relative silence. Isolated. In the woods, it was
an overload to his senses. And what she was offering
was a chance to take that energy at the center of his
guts, and pour it all out.

He had been so en garde about her manipulating
him. But she was a goddess. He had that realization
when he had seen her tonight.

He did not often think of Freya. He had let go of
the idea of deities so long ago.

And yet he could remember a story. Whispered to
him before he fell asleep at night.

He couldn't remember who had told him. His
mother, a nanny? But when Fern had come in wearing that gold gown, he had thought of Freya.

That soft voice inside of him whispering about the promise of Freya's afterlife.

It is one thing to die in battle. It is another to die for those you love. And any soldier who goes to battle with love in his heart is dying for that love. Freya weeps for her husband. Because she separated from him. She understands the pain of love being lost. And that is why her field is reserved for those who wish to meet again with their heart's desire after death.

Such a strange thing. The memory had been so strong. It was still.

And it made him want to draw closer to Fern.

It certainly made him feel as if he didn't want to resist.

No. He had no desire to resist.

He also couldn't wait. He wrapped his arm around her waist and pressed her body up to his.

It was familiar now. And yet gloriously undiscovered.

He lowered his head and kissed her. The taste of her mouth better than the cake. And he had decided he very much liked cake.

He kissed her. Deep and hard, and with a ferocity he had never before given to a lover. Because he had never felt such an intense, specific need before. It had to be her. It had to be.

He held her face as he kissed her. As he tasted her, his tongue sliding against hers.

And then when they parted, she looked up at him, those green eyes clear. "Yes. Take me to bed."

"I have questions for you first," he said, a strange

sensation gripping his stomach. Concern. For her. He no longer felt that he was in danger of being manipulated by her. Because this was not manipulation. It was far too honest. But he required things to also be clear.

"Yes?" She looked uncertain.

"Why is it that you've decided you want me?"

"I don't know that I decided that I wanted you. I simply do."

"You know that I'm not staking a claim on your body by keeping you here as my wife. You are not obligated to give yourself to me."

"I know that."

"You have told me that no one in your life has ever cared for your choices. You told me that you felt like all these men made a claim on your sexuality, me included. I didn't even think of it that way. I…"

She touched his face. "I believe you. I know that you were practically raised by wolves. And I know that…I wasn't a person to you. I was an ideal. A goal. And I would be more offended by that except I also understand that you even see yourself as a person. As a man. You see yourself as a symbol of revolution. As a king, but not as a man."

"True," he said, the words rising rough in his throat. "All true."

"But I see you as a man. And I want for you to feel like a man tonight. I want you to let go of everything. Of your idea of duty, and honor. Take what you want. And I'll take what I want."

"I don't understand."

"There is nothing to understand. I spent the last three years in a convent, and even I know that."

"Sex isn't confusing. Need isn't confusing. It's simply an appetite."

"This isn't an appetite. There's something between us. Even when you were furious at me in the library, you wanted me. Even when I was running from you, when you brought me up on the back of that horse, I felt…your heat. Part of me wanted to lean into your strength, rather than run away from it—I can't explain it. But we have this time. This marriage. Why can't we enjoy it?"

"You want me," he said. Because everything else she was saying was difficult to hold onto. In his lust-addled brain it was moving through too quickly.

"Yes, Ragnar. I want you. Not because you kidnapped me, and not because we got married. If I had seen you across a crowded ballroom, if you had always been the king of this country, if you had been in the life you should've had, and I had been in mine, I would've wanted you."

She wanted him. She was choosing him. Of all the limited choices that Fern had been able to make in her life, he now counted as one of them. There had been spare few pleasures in his life that he could remember. Only small moments of joy.

But this stood out as one of the greatest. One of the most profound. It was nothing like the potential for satisfying an appetite. It was something deeper. Something that reached through the garden walls around his heart and touched him.

Touched his soul.

He hadn't even thought it was possible. He wasn't even sure that he retained a soul. In much the same way he had lost his faith in anything divine.

But then, he kissed her. And it was like looking into the heavens. An experience beyond anything he had ever had before. She was a virgin.

And yet he might as well have been.

He had always looked at sex as something divorced of any emotional connection. He had honed his skills, because he did not believe in using a person for pleasure without giving it in return. But it was only his body involved. While now everything felt locked in. Everything felt engaged.

And then every pass of her lips over his, of his tongue against hers, felt like something new.

He lifted her up, sweeping her into his arms, the way that he had done on the Isle of Skye when he had plucked her off the ground. Only this time, he did not put her on the back of his horse. This time, he held her against his chest as he carried her down the long corridor, and to the spiral staircase that led to his chambers.

The room was sparse, and he still was not in the habit of sleeping on the bed. When he opened the door, his bedroll was still on the floor beside the large canopy bed, and his eyes went to it, even though he wished she wouldn't notice.

"What is that?"

"I'm not accustomed to sleeping in a bed. I spent most of my life sleeping on the floor. And then on the ground outside."

"Oh but that's…"

"It's all right. I have been saving this bed. I needed a reason to use it. And you have given me that."

She smiled, and it was like something had been lit up inside of him. "That was almost funny."

"I feel almost amused."

With her lips still curved into a smile she wrapped her arms around his neck and kissed him again. He growled, laying her down in the center of the bed. The mattress was soft. And so was she. He looked down at her, at all that glorious gold over her beautiful body. He touched her face, and for a moment, he could only stare in reverence at all of her beauty.

She truly was glorious.

Not a conquest. Even better than that, she was giving herself to him. Joyfully.

She had chosen him.

That reality echoed inside of him, stronger than any heartbeat. Stronger than anything.

If this was joy, then he could understand why people threw away their duty, their honor, their everything to pursue it.

He himself was unfamiliar with the feeling. He had felt something like it when they had finally managed to reclaim the country, but even then it had not been pure joy. Because on the other side of the victory lay a long road ahead.

While this was all about the moment. Not a race to the finish line, not the beginning of the next step. He intended to take his time with her. To devour her. To luxuriate in this.

"What do you know about sex?" he asked.

"I have not spent these past years in the woods like you. I think I know quite a bit about it."

"Yes? You think?"

"I'm not ignorant."

"You were in a convent."

"Not because of any great pious thoughts on my part. I was in a convent because I was being hidden away. But I wasn't reading the catechism."

"Were you reading manuals about sex?"

"No. In fact, I deliberately didn't think about it. It's why it took me some time to realize that I was attracted to you."

"Is that so?"

"Well. That and you being my kidnapper."

He chuckled. "I can see how that might be a barrier."

"I told you. I felt like I had been given away. It made it so that my fantasies weren't even mine. Because if I thought too much about sex, if I thought too much about any of that, then I would have to think about it with…him."

"And of course you didn't want that."

"No. Of course I didn't. So yes, I know about it. I know plenty, but I wouldn't say that I'm…"

"I'll teach you."

He lowered his head and kissed her neck and she arched beneath him, grasping his shoulders.

He growled, and she gasped. He raised his head and looked at her. "Did I frighten you?"

She shook her head. "No. I… I like it."

"I am not a civilized man. Perhaps if you had chosen differently, you would not get a man who growls."

"If he doesn't growl then I don't want him."

Then she kissed him, and he kissed her back, luxuriating in the feel of her soft mouth on his.

Then, the warrior in her came out. He could feel her nerves leaving her body, could feel all the resolute determination within her as she kissed him, his face, his neck.

As if she was the one mounting a seduction.

"Let me," he said.

Even though he knew that she wouldn't. Because she had to fight him; it was what made her feel alive. He knew that much.

One warrior recognized another.

He pulled away from her, stripped off his jacket and then unbuttoned his shirt. Then he cast both onto the floor, before getting off the bed momentarily to take off the rest of his clothes. Her eyes went around, her focus going immediately to his cock.

She bit her lip, her reaction much more so one of interest than of nerves.

She rose up on her knees, her dress pooled around her like a golden puddle, her hair falling forward. Divine. Pagan. All at once.

She leaned in, and pressed a kiss to his hip.

A short grunt rose up in the back of his throat.

"I told you—"

"And I told you that this was my choice. So let me have what I want."

She leaned in, sliding her tongue along the length

of his arousal. And then she parted her lips, taking him in, a feminine gasp escaping her lips as she released him a moment later. And then she went back, teasing him, tormenting him, lavishing him with attention.

He gripped her hair, watching as her mouth slid up and down on his rod, watching as she took her pleasure by giving him pleasure.

She made whimpering sounds, sweet, tormented noises that told him she was delighting in this as much as he was.

"Good girl," he growled.

Her cheeks went pink as she continued to suck him, and he felt himself reaching the end of his composure. The end of his control.

"Enough, my Freya. Or I will deny you the loss of your virginity by losing myself."

Her lips curved into a smile, those wicked lips, swollen now with need. "So you liked it?"

"If I liked it any more, then this would be over."

"I've never done it before."

"I assumed. But not because it wasn't good. Only because… You are mine, aren't you? Entirely? You have never kissed another man, never touched another man. You've never even wanted one, have you?"

It was suddenly imperative that he know that. That he be absolutely certain that her need was for him, and for him alone.

"Yes," she whispered. "You are the only one."

"Good."

Everything in life that had once been his had been

taken from him. In some way, it healed him to know that she had come to him, and she was his. It was that simple.

And in two years if she went her own way, and went to another man, he would still have been her first.

And right now, she was his. It was all that mattered.

She reached behind her back, as if she were reaching for the zipper of her dress. "No," he growled. "That's my task to complete."

He lifted her up, and repositioned her so that she was sitting on the edge of the bed. Then he gripped one of the straps of her dress and pushed it down, so that it fell, loosening her bodice. He did the same to the other side. The diaphanous fabric was still covering her breasts, but had exposed more of her ample cleavage.

He left her just like that, her hair a wild tangle, the image she made that of a feral, gorgeous creature.

Then he got down on his knees, and pushed up the hem of that skirt, exposing her slim ankles, her calves. Pushing the skirt up until he could see her thighs, until he saw the sheer panties that she had on beneath the dress. He could see the shadow of dark curls beneath the diaphanous fabric, and his body throbbed in anticipation of having her.

But no. He would not claim her like that. He would not sink himself into her without preamble no matter how badly he wanted it. He had to bring her to pleasure first. He had to give her everything. And then some.

He hooked his fingers into the sides of her underwear, and pulled them down her legs, opening her thighs so that he could see her glistening folds.

She was art, this woman. And he would worship at her altar, above any other.

How could such pagan beauty exist? Someone so strong, resilient, regal and yet hewn from the earth.

He would never have thought that a princess would appeal to him like this. He would've thought that he was the kind of man so lost to the civilized world that he could not want a woman like her, and yet. It was as though she had been brought forth from the forest just for him.

He leaned in, inhaling the scent of her arousal before he pressed a kiss to her inner thigh.

She gasped, and he pressed forward, licking her right where she was wet and needy for him.

She gasped, her hands going around his hair as he began to devour her.

How long had it been since he had tasted a woman? It didn't even matter what the answer was. Because no woman had ever been her. No woman had ever appealed to him in this way.

No one had ever reached the heart of him. But she did.

Like she had reached up into the sky and brought the stars down among them. Like she had made magic between them with nothing more than the wave of her hand.

He kissed her there. Teased her, tormented her, and then he pushed a finger deep inside of her tight passage, stretching her, trying to prepare her for what came next. But what came next didn't matter. What mattered the most was what was happening now. What mattered the most was him giving her all the pleasure that she could ever receive.

He pressed a second finger inside of her, and she moved her hands to his shoulders, her fingernails digging into his skin.

He sucked her clit deep into his mouth, as he continued to thrust his fingers within her, and she gasped his name, tightening her thighs on either side of his face as she came explosively against his mouth.

He kept going. Because there was no reason for him to stop. Because there was no reason she couldn't have more.

Because she had been given so little in her life, because people had shown so little care for her feelings. For what she wanted, and him among them. He owed her penance. He owed her pleasure.

And he would forfeit his own desires for this, any moment.

Every day.

Her back arched up off the bed again, a second orgasm tearing through her as she curled her hands around the bedspread.

"Yes," he growled, lifting his head and kissing her thigh again.

"Beautiful."

He looked up at her, and she touched his face, her eyes gone dark, like the deepest part of the forest.

"Ragnar…"

"You are mine," he said. "This body is mine. But only to do as it pleases you. That is my calling. It is my right. To claim you, but in the way that makes you scream my name."

She was trembling when he stood, his body so hard it hurt now, and reached around to undo the zipper on her dress. She reached out and gripped his shaft, squeezing as he let her dress fall around her waist, exposing her breasts.

They were beautiful. So much lovelier than he had even imagined they might be.

"They would've written songs about you," he said. "Back in the conquering days."

"Would they have also stolen me from my home and brought me to a strange land?"

"That is what I did. I can hardly expect the barbarians of old to behave any differently."

"But the song is supposed to be the consolation?"

"The song is attribute. An offering. To a goddess."

"Oh."

He reached out and took her hand, had her stand, and her dress fell to the floor. She was completely naked in front of him, wearing nothing but her gold shoes now. He knelt down, and began to undo the buckles.

She watched intently as he did. "Because two things can be true," he said. "I can claim you, but you can claim me. I might be the king. But I will be on my knees before you."

"And will you take me?"

"Yes." He stood, and wrapped his arm around her,

brought her up against his body so that they were pressed together, totally naked, holding onto each other. And he kissed her just like that, luxuriating in the feel of it. The decadence of being there, being naked, and having time.

To kiss her all over. To take her as he wished.

As she wished.

"No, my lady," he said, picking her up and wrapping her legs around his waist and then climbing onto the bed, laying her on her back at the center of the mattress. "I will have you."

He put his hand between her thighs, pushed two fingers in her again as he felt how wet and ready she was.

Then he kissed her mouth, her neck, lowered his head to take one nipple into his mouth and sucked hard.

She arched up off the mattress and then he positioned himself at the entrance of her body, and thrust deep inside of her in one smooth stroke.

"Ragnar," she cried, her internal muscles pulsing, tightening around him. She did not seem to be in pain. Rather she seemed to be having the aftershocks of another release. He began to move, not allowing that trembling to subside as he staked his claim over and over again.

Her wet heat drove him to the edge. Made him feel more beast than man, but for a better reason than ever before. Not because he was being stripped of every comfort, every bit of humanity, but because he was acting only on instinct. Only on need.

He could feel her getting close. Another orgasm building within her. And his own was about to steal every last bit of his control. He put his hand between them, brushing his thumb over her clit as he continued to thrust inside of her.

A short cry escaped her mouth, and he drove himself into her quickly, chasing his own satisfaction. And when it hit, with all the force of a pack of wolves, gripped him around his throat and left him gasping for air, he cried out her name: "Fern."

His Fern.

"Mine," he growled, resting his forehead against hers.

They held each other for a long moment after.

Then he moved away from her, and tucked her against his side. He pushed her hair away from her face. He had never done this before.

Never held a woman in the aftermath of pleasure.

"Why is there sadness in Freya?"

Her voice was soft, in the silence of the room.

"She's sad because her husband left her. He's roaming the earth, and she's waiting for him back home. But he isn't there."

"My husband is here," she said, putting her hand over his.

He felt as if he had been stabbed, clean through the chest.

The sweetness, the softness of her words nearly unmanning him.

"Yes," he said. "I am. I will never leave this place."

In truth, in the future, he would be more like Freya.

Tasked with guarding a particular place, and unable to follow her as she went on to make her choices. To live her life.

But she could be unburdened of all of this. She could be free.

And he would rejoice for her.

He hadn't cared at first. Not at all. He hadn't seen her as a person, just as she had said. She had been an ideal. A symbol. Something that he had thought might be useful.

But not a person.

She had in this short space of time become the person that he knew best. She had become someone who mattered. And he couldn't remember the last time a person had mattered to him. An idea, yes. People as a group, yes. But not a person. One that he wanted to know. To touch, to kiss, to keep with him.

"I guess I'll always know where to find you," she whispered. Then she leaned in and kissed his hand.

"Yes," he said. "You will."

CHAPTER TEN

FERN WOKE IN the early hours of the morning, and it took her some time to remember what had happened the night before. She had slept with Ragnar.

That was when she became aware of her body. Of her surroundings. She ached in interesting places. And she was lying in a bed different than her own. But she was alone.

She frowned, she looked around and then sat up. Then she peered down over the edge of the mattress and saw that he was there. On the floor, on that awful bedroll.

Her chest tightened.

It wasn't as simple for him as leaving that life behind. It had left an indelible mark on him. He couldn't even fully enjoy comfortable things.

She wanted to tear down the walls of the castle, to unmake the world and remake it for him. If only she were a goddess. If only she had that kind of power. If only things were different.

She had said to him that if she had seen him at a ball, and she had been free to approach him, and he had been free to approach her, then they would've ended up together. They would have too.

But they didn't have the option of finding each other in that ideal space. They didn't have the option for being those people. They were Ragnar and Fern. And they were shaped by the things that had happened to them. Deeply. In ways that were not quite so simple to fix.

If they were, this man wouldn't be sleeping on the floor when he lived in a whole palace.

She couldn't make that pain go away for him. But she could join him where he was.

She climbed out of bed, and lowered herself down onto the floor, taking the blanket with her as she lay alongside of him, only able to claim just a small sliver of the bedroll. He startled, sitting up like he was ready for battle. And then he looked down at her.

"What are you doing?"

"I wasn't going to leave you down here to sleep by yourself."

"You don't need to sleep on the floor with me."

"Then why are you sleeping on the floor?"

"It is none of your concern."

"It is my concern, though. You are my concern."

"And why is that? Because you're going to leave this place. You're going to leave me."

That life, the one that she had envisioned for herself after this, felt different now. It didn't seem as clear. It didn't seem as sharp.

"But two years are not nothing," she said. "Think of the three years you've been back here. Think of all that has changed. Think of all the more that will be changed by the time our agreement comes to an end. Maybe you'll be sleeping in a bed."

He sat up. "Maybe."

She sat up with him, grabbing hold of his bicep. He had gotten dressed, which she didn't like. "I'm all into this. For the time that we have."

"You do not have to sleep on the floor."

"You could sleep in the bed."

"I don't like to sleep too deeply. In case something happens."

Her heart hurt. "Were you potentially under attack when you were waiting to take the country back?"

"No. Earlier. That was when things were truly dangerous."

"You talked about it before. It was your nanny that helped you escape?"

"That's my understanding. Because I don't remember. But I was told later by the family that cared for me."

"Your nanny didn't continue to take care of you?"

"No. She was afraid that she would be too easy to track down. She left me with some distant relatives."

"And they knew that you were the heir to the throne but they treated you like a servant?"

"They always told me it was for my own good. As I said, my identity was never hidden from me. And I knew. I knew my name. I knew that I was the king. With both of my parents dead, I knew. But it meant nothing to me. So it seemed perfectly reasonable that they had me sleep in the barn. I used to guard the animals."

"Oh God, you've been without a bed for all this time?"

"Yes. It became something of a habit."

He sounded completely remote. Emotionless.

"Doesn't it make you angry? Shouldn't someone have taken you and treated you like family?"

He shook his head. "I already told you. Family doesn't mean anything to me because I don't remember mine. How can I miss what I don't understand? And it was what I needed to make change. I left that situation when I was fifteen. I got work washing dishes in a restaurant. That was when I first heard rumblings of desires for revolution. Those people didn't know who I was, but I paid attention to every word. Gradually, I realized that the national mood was for a change in leadership. And I realized that I was the person who could bring about change. But I had to. Because a new leader would have to prove himself. It wouldn't be so simple as taking things over. But for me it would be."

"It took you seventeen years from that point?"

"Yes. Because you can't go around announcing that you are the long-lost heir."

"I don't suppose you can."

"No. You have to be very careful about who you talk to. About who you reveal your plans to. I started with the other man I washed dishes with. Soren."

"And he's your right-hand man now."

"Yes. We began to build an army. Using a whisper

network. We were like Robin Hood's band of thieves. Or like Vikings of old. We had a few bases of operation. One deep in the woods, which you have no doubt picked up on. And another in the city. In the capital. Very close to the palace. That was how we began to infiltrate the military. And all during that time I educated myself. On government, on the economy. On leadership. I read about the way that my father ran the country. And I tried to figure out the mistakes that I thought he had made. How he had gone wrong. Because something must've been wrong, or those people would not have happily supported a coup." He lowered his head slightly. "Even then I could not remember him. He was words on the page to me, nothing more."

She nodded slowly. "So most of your life you've devoted to this."

"Yes. It was much better than being a servant boy with no family and no future."

"Still. It sounds like a very hard existence."

"The only kind of existence available to anyone in Asland for the last twenty-five years has been a hard existence. Mine is not unique. That's why when I meet my people I tell them not to give me deference of any kind. I'm not unique. We have all suffered. And we must all move forward together."

"But can you heal?"

Her heart was pounding heavily, painfully.

"I've never thought about it."

"Can you sleep in a bed. Can you enjoy cake? Can you let yourself rest? Sleep? You're in a castle surrounded by guards."

"This is the same palace that my parents were killed in, Fern. I can no more sleep deeply here than I can anywhere."

The horror of that truth washed over her. Of course he didn't feel safe here. It had proven to be unsafe. It was the same palace where his family had been killed, but it was also the same palace he had reclaimed all those years later. He knew every weakness. He had exploited those weaknesses. And he had been the victim of those weaknesses. Why would he ever feel safe?

She hated it. That life had been so appalling to him.

"It is so important to you," he said softly. "To try to make everything okay. You wish to erase the bad things in your own life as well—that is what you see ahead of you when you think about a life filled with choices, is it not?"

"I guess so."

"But they have happened. These bad things. We cannot make ourselves unchanged by them."

It was so like what she had been thinking when she had first seen him down there on the floor. That it didn't matter if they would have found each other without all the trauma. Because the trauma was real. Because it had shaped them into who they were.

But it was just hard to accept that they might need it. She was sure that wasn't true. Nobody deserved to be treated the way that he had. And she felt certain that she didn't deserve what had happened to her— even though in the end she had been safe.

"You're a warrior," he said.

"Excuse me?"

"You are like me, Fernanda. You are a warrior. A great strategist. I've seen it."

"You said that I was manipulative."

"I take it back. Because I see you differently now. You had to be strong and smart, you had to learn how to operate in a way that keeps you safe, but also advances your cause. You are a warrior like me. A true warrior does not fear battle scars. A warrior understands that it is part of battle."

"I never wanted to be in battle."

"It doesn't matter sometimes. In fact, it doesn't matter most of the time. We are not asked what life we would like to live. We are given this life. We are given our fate. But we have to decide what to do with it. But we do not run from it."

"And where do we start making choices?"

"We are making them. Now. Do you think you really have not been making choices all this time? You have been. The way that you learned to be, and the way that you acted, that was a choice. What you did with your time at the convent, that was a choice. The way that you used all that you had learned from your father to get me to grant you your eventual freedom. That was a choice. What we did last night. And what we are doing now."

She looked down at her hands.

"We are stronger for what we've been through. Stronger for the battles that we have fought. Don't you see?"

She took a shuddering breath. "Yes."

"Now. Today, I think we should go out into the country."

"The country?"

"Not just the country. Our country. I wish to speak to the people."

"Okay. Then that's what we'll do."

And as she got herself ready, she could only think about what he had said. When they were in the car that was carrying them toward the town square, she was still pondering it.

"Yes?"

"Nothing. I'm just thinking." She looked out the window, at the view of the city. People going to work. Smiling. Laughing. All of those people had a particular set of circumstances that they were given. Fair and unfair.

And they were making what they could of those circumstances. In that sense, she could understand what he had been saying to her all this time. About choice being an illusion. No one had infinite choices. They had the circumstances they were given. People that they were responsible for.

Just as he was. Responsible for this entire country.

"You were thinking very loudly."

"I'm not trying to."

"You might as well tell me."

"It's silly. And in fact, I imagine that you think I'm a silly girl entirely. You're right. What I wanted was to be normal. Or whatever I thought of as normal. I wanted to be able to leave my father's house, and become somebody that I wasn't raised to be. Become somebody who hadn't lived the first eighteen years of her life cloistered in a palace, promised to marry a man that she didn't care about. Someone who hadn't been treated like she didn't matter, even while she was surrounded by luxury. I wanted to live like I had sprung fully formed from the convent, and go on my merry way. But I can't be separate from those experiences. I can't be someone who didn't have them. And you're also right, that I can't make…any choice that I want. I have a shared responsibility with you now. For these people."

"I do not think you're silly," he said. "Most people want to be happy."

"You don't?"

"It's not something I've ever considered. Whether or not I was happy."

"That makes me even sillier. You realize that, right? I have been thinking to myself that we actually have quite a bit in common. That we both spent so much of our lives lonely, but I never had to worry about my survival. When I saw you sleeping on the floor like that, I realized…you never feel safe, do you?"

"That isn't true. I am entirely able to defend myself, and that makes me feel safe. But no, sleeping deeply doesn't entirely appeal to me."

Their conversation was ended because their car parked against the curb at the town square, and they got out. "Is this what we're doing? We're just…"

Their security detail was with them. Soren first and foremost. And now she knew and understood that he was Ragnar's lifelong, trusted friend. Even if he wouldn't call him a friend. That was a very male thing. Quite literally spent seventeen years in the company of someone, and waged a literal war with him, but still not quite think of him as a friend.

"Let us speak to our people."

It didn't take long for them to be lost in a crowd. A crush of people that were excited to meet them. There were photos being taken, flashes on cameras and cell phones being shoved in their faces. Through it all, Ragnar remained completely calm.

Fern clung to him like she was afraid she was going to lose her grip, and be separated from him. The idea of being separated from him frightened her.

But he held her tightly, and while people did get close to them, they never made physical contact, because Ragnar's demeanor discouraged them from getting too close.

There was a benefit to having a husband who looked like a Viking warrior of old.

They finished with the crowd of people there at the city center, and then got back in their car, and began to drive toward a nearby village. She hadn't seen this much of the country yet.

The buildings were an interesting mix of clean, modern lines, and old structures. There were black churches, standing stark against the countryside.

"There are so many trees here," she commented. "Iceland doesn't have trees."

"Yes. The legend is that the Vikings cut down all the trees in Iceland and they never grew again. Personally, I don't believe that. They are a renewable resource after all."

"And what do you think it is?"

"Giants? Trolls?"

"I didn't think that you believed in the divine."

"I don't. However, that does not mean that I don't believe in trolls and giants."

She blinked. "It doesn't?"

"Of course not. Anyone descended from Norsemen believes in trolls and giants. You are foolish not to."

"I didn't realize."

There was never as big of a crowd as the first one they drew in the capital city, but people were friendly, and greeted them with enthusiasm everywhere they went. They stopped in a pub, where they had fish and chips and cider. She had never done anything like this. She had never walked around in and among people. She had either been cloistered in a palace, or cloistered in a convent.

Maybe this was what her life would be like when she went to make her own way. Maybe she would live in a village, and she would simply talk to people.

Except of course they would all know who she was. Well, maybe not all. Just because they were well-known in this part of Europe didn't mean they would be well-known everywhere.

"We have been invited to stay in one of the oldest hotels in the country," he said.

"We have?"

"Yes," he said. He gestured toward the end of the street. "That large stone building there. It was once a place where royalty stayed. And I suppose it can be again."

"I would like that."

And they would of course get the same room, and it would be…

Just thinking about it made her warm.

When they arrived at the room, she took her phone out, and began to look at headlines on a news site. And was shocked to discover that they were the focus of many of them.

"Look at this," she said, bringing her phone over to him. "There are…hundreds and hundreds of pictures of today."

"You seem alarmed."

"I didn't realize…"

"You are very popular," he said. "After the ball we received glowing press about you."

"I didn't see it."

"Why not?"

"I was distracted by the sex."

"Ah. I was also distracted by that. But I received communication about your popularity early this morning."

"And you didn't share it with me?"

"I didn't have a chance to. But now I am."

"It isn't only me that's popular," she said. "You are too. A king of the people. Unlike the evil dictator before you. And unlike…" She frowned. "Unlike your father."

She turned the screen of her phone off, almost like she was trying to protect him.

"I know," he said.

"What?"

"I already know that my father was not considered a man of the people. I told you that I spent seventeen years trying to figure out how to be the leader that this country needed. Part of that was finding out what had made it ripe for revolution in the first place."

"You don't have any memories of your father, only these…pieces written by other people?"

"I spent a fair amount of time talking to people who remembered him. He was seen as decadent. Out of touch." He frowned. "It feels foolish to have to ask. To not know."

"I should've asked about that before I went and threw a ball."

"Nothing about your ball seemed decadent or out of touch. My father would never have welcomed the citizens of the country. At least, that is my understanding. He certainly never would've walked through the town square."

"You're trying to counteract his reputation."

"Yes. I would be foolish not to."

Yet again, she saw that inability for him to feel certainty. For him to feel like anything was fixed or secure.

Because in his experience, it wasn't.

"You're your own man," she said. "All of these articles recognize it."

She looked around the room, properly, for the first time since they had arrived. It was lovely. Filled with cultural charm. That modern, Scandinavian type of design, mixed with more ornate old-world art and wallpaper.

But she didn't care about the surroundings. She only cared about him.

"I am whatever the people need me to be."

"Is it so impossible for you to let yourself be human?"

"Yes. It is."

"Let yourself be a man, Ragnar."

"I have to be better than that. I'm a king."

"Not in here. If I can give you one thing over the next two years, I want to give you that. With me, you don't have to be a king. With me, you can simply be a man."

Driven by the impulse that was making her heart beat faster, she reached around and unzipped the dress that she was wearing. Let it fall away from her body. Let it fall all the way to the floor. "I don't need you to be a symbol of anything. I only need you to be a man."

CHAPTER ELEVEN

HIS EYES WENT DARK. And she could see that he wasn't going to argue. Wasn't going to resist.

Instead he crossed the space between them and pulled her into his arms. "What is it you want exactly?"

"You," she said, moving her hand down to cup his arousal. "I don't need you to be on guard. I only need you to be Ragnar."

She could see him fighting a battle inside of himself. She could see that he wanted what she was offering. That he wanted to surrender to her. To his need.

She could also see that he was desperate to hang onto that guarded component of himself.

It wasn't just a sense of self-protection. It was more than that. It wasn't only about being there for his country. The way that he had depersonalized himself was essential to his survival, and she could see that in the tortured lines of his face.

She craved his surrender. But she did not crave his destruction.

He was strong. He had cultivated that strength over

years of being the man his country needed. Of being the man those around him needed. A myth. A legend.

And yet there was more to it.

She sensed it now; she just couldn't figure out exactly what it was.

But he was a man with razor wire around his heart, and she had identified that from the beginning.

When he had accused her of manipulating him, it had been coming from a place of self-preservation. But why?

Yes, there were so many reasons in his past, but she didn't think that they were the reasons that he had given her.

She didn't think he was lying. But she did think that he was an incomplete man. A man missing pieces of his past, a man who didn't know how to embrace the future. Not apart from duty and honor.

Slowly, she reached out and put her hand on his chest. A short growl escaped his lips, and then she reached up and touched his face. Stroked his cheekbone, down his jaw. "You don't have to fight a war right now. Just be mine."

She was wearing a pair of purple high heels, and matching underwear, and she watched as his gaze darkened. As desire propelled him forward.

"Ragnar," she said. "All you have to be with me is you."

It was as if he lost control entirely then. His growl was deeper, more feral, more sustained as he reached out and wrapped his arms around her, drawing her up against him and kissing her with all the ferocity of a man on the front lines of the battlefield.

He claimed her. Forced her lips open then thrust his tongue deep. There was an honesty to this that soothed something inside of her.

But perhaps it had always been that way with him.

Because he might be a man who didn't know himself, he might be a man who didn't know how to explain all of the things he'd been through or all of the things that he believed in, thought and felt, but he was a man of integrity. A man who did exactly what he said he was going to do. A man to be proud of.

She had never been proud of any of the men she had ever known. She found them selfish. Manipulative. Diabolical.

Men who sowed lies and acted like they might grow something other than a poisoned crop.

But not Ragnar.

He was a man who had survived. A man who had fought, all for the good of others, and never for the good of himself. It made her want to worship him. To give him everything. All of herself.

It made her want to fling herself upon his altar and worship.

So she did. With her lips, her tongue. She offered him supplication in the form of her neck exposed for him, to kiss, to bite. In the form of kisses that she spread across his chest, as she worked to remove his clothes, as she dropped to her knees and took him deep into her mouth.

As she gave him all of the evidence of her longing.

All of her desire.

She needed him.

And she wanted him to know that.

Thinking about the isolation that he had lived in filled her with despair.

Who had ever been here for this man? If anyone ever had, he couldn't even remember it. So she had to build new memories for him. Feelings of warmth. Of connection. Of family.

You can't leave him.

She pushed that thought aside. She continued to pleasure him with her mouth, her tongue, her hands.

As she drove him to the brink, took him to the edge.

As she gave to him, wholly and completely.

"Fern," he growled, his hands in her hair. He was trying to stop her from finishing it this way.

But she would not be stopped.

He had said it himself. She was a warrior. Maybe of another variety than him, but made from the same mettle all the same.

And so she continued. Sucking him in deep until his hips arched forward, until he surrendered. Until he gave her the victory that she craved, on a hoarse cry, spilling himself down her throat.

And now she knew what it was like to win in battle. Because this time, she truly had.

He let out a long, ragged breath, releasing his hold.

She stood up, and took his hand, leading him over to the bed. She stripped off all of her remaining clothes, and got beneath the blankets beside him, stroking his chest with her fingertips.

"There will be more," he said, an iron promise in his voice.

"I know. But there doesn't need to be right this second."

"You are a handful," he said.

"Yes. I've been told that. Every tutor that I ever had despaired of me. Because my mind was always several steps ahead, and I thought most of what I was being taught was stupid. I'm all for diplomacy, as you know. But what I'm not all for is empty manners that might be pretty on the surface, but serve nothing and no one beneath."

"No. You don't strike me as someone who takes kindly to dishonesty."

"I'm not. That's why I got irritated when you said I was manipulative."

"You are not dishonest," he said. "I misspoke. It was only that I thought you might get me to change in some way, and for a while I was resisting that."

"And are you still resisting it?"

He looked up at the ceiling. "I suppose I've never had to change around other people. I was tasked with growing myself into a leader, and I did. Inflexibility was a hallmark of the good that I was doing, and so change feels like the mortal enemy of that. But you are right. It was a different time. Different than when I was growing up. And my job is now different. What I wanted was for you to teach me how to put on a performance. I didn't want you to truly change me. But I'm learning things from you, Fern. Whether I set out to do so or not."

"Oh, that must bother you so."

"It doesn't bother me. Not anymore. Not now, anyway. Perhaps tomorrow it will."

"I do think that we both grew up quite lonely. I was surrounded by people, but they didn't know me. They didn't care for me. Not as I was."

"They only saw what they could make you into."

"Yes. But still, I... You grew up with no one. Did no one ever care if you were hungry? Cold?"

He shook his head. "No."

"I wonder if that's why you don't know how to show any sort of care or compassion to yourself. Because nobody ever showed it to you. No one taught you that it mattered. If you were comfortable. If you felt good or bad or scared or upset..."

"I've never been afraid."

"Never?"

"No. To tell you the truth, I have always assumed that whatever happened that day in the palace frightened me so much it was like a fire had been held to the part of myself that once was able to feel fear, and scalded away all of the nerve endings. Left it completely dead. I have felt vigilance. A deep sense of protectiveness for my people. But not fear. Not for my own self. Not for much of anything. It is a gift."

"Is it? Even when it prevents you from feeling everything else?"

"I don't feel anything else. Or rather, I don't miss what I don't feel. How can you, when you have no idea what to expect?"

That must be because he didn't have any context

for himself. He didn't remember the first eight years of his life, and she couldn't imagine what that would do to somebody. How badly that might impact you.

There were things that she wished she couldn't remember from her childhood. But it was different to having a whole swath of yourself entirely erased.

"Just because you don't know it doesn't mean it isn't important. Like eating cake. You might not have known that you were missing out, but you were."

"And yet, it isn't an important thing. If I had never had it, I would not miss it."

"But doesn't it bother you? Knowing that there is so much out there that you haven't experienced?"

"No. It does bother you, though, doesn't it?"

There was deep compassion in his eyes, nothing dismissive. It was entirely different from all the times before when they had talked about what she wanted from life. And the great irony was, she didn't feel like she wanted it any longer. Not in the same way.

Yes, there were things that she was curious about. There was the potential for a life that she might enjoy out there, but it was only a possibility. It wasn't real. Not in the same way that he was. Not in the same way that this was.

"I think it bothered me so much because I felt like I didn't get to choose," she said.

The truth of that rang inside of her like a bell. So clear, so bright. "I felt like because I didn't have a say in my own future that it seemed unfair. That there was such a big wide world out there and I would never get to explore it. I don't feel that same urgency now."

She didn't feel like the walls were closing in. She didn't feel like every step was laid out before her before she ever got a chance to choose it.

She wanted to stay with him. He had agreed to let her go.

Maybe she was just a contrarian.

She didn't think so.

It was like what he'd said. Initially, she had been determined to come out of this without changing. Then she had begun to open herself up to the idea of living while she was here.

But living meant changing. It meant growing in understanding. Of herself, of what she wanted. Of who she was.

It meant being affected.

She had been fighting that for so much of her life. Resisting allowing her father to alter who she was. To dent her spirit in any way.

He was right; she had been resisting being changed or affected by her trauma. But it had happened. That part of her life was real.

Just the same as she could allow herself to be changed by this. And she had. She could change what she wanted. It didn't make her a failure. It didn't mean that she was losing a fight.

She wasn't giving in.

Not to anything other than what she wanted. What she was moving toward. There was something good in that. Something powerful in it. In feeling. In wanting. In accepting.

"After this the world will be yours."

She wanted to correct him. She wanted to tell him that she was going to stay. But the words got stuck in her throat. He was changing. He had admitted to that. He had even said that he didn't hate the idea of it anymore. That was the beginning of something.

But she was afraid. Afraid to push him too hard too fast. Though what she thought he might do, she couldn't say. He had been intent on taking her as a wife forever.

Forever.

Was that really what she wanted?

She felt something, something big and fierce in the center of her chest, and when she looked at him it was nearly painful.

When she touched him, it felt like coming home. In a way that home had never been.

She didn't have words. Not to speak, not even to form inside of herself to try to create an understanding. So she leaned over and she kissed him, letting the blankets fall away, so that her bare skin could press up against his.

He wrapped his arm around her waist, brought her over the top of him, cupping her face as he kissed her with all of the pent-up desire inside of him.

She sat up, and looked down at him, her hair enveloping them both in a dark, tangled curtain.

She felt alive. She felt free. She felt like she belonged to him, and it was nothing like being owned. Because she felt as if he belonged to her too. As if she was the only person who might totally understand.

Even if she didn't today, maybe someday she would. She wanted to.

She wanted to change around him. Wanted to re-form herself in his arms.

She couldn't make him want the same.

But she felt…

She bent down and kissed him, and he growled, gripping her hips and moving her down so that her wet heat came into contact with the blunt head of his arousal. She gasped. And then she arched her hips backward, taking him in deep from her position on top of him. She moaned as he filled her, slowly, completely. And then she began to writhe above him. A claiming of her own.

Mine.

Mine.

Mine.

Yes.

She gripped his shoulders, letting her head fall back as she established a rhythm that drove them both mad.

She carried them both to the brink.

This man. He was something. He was everything.

She moaned, shuddering as her orgasm claimed her unexpectedly. And then he growled, reversing their positions so that he was on top of her, driving into her. His powerful hold was like chains, but she never wanted to break free of them.

It was the beauty of him. The paradox of him.

A conqueror, who never made her feel conquered.

Who only made her feel stronger. More herself. More alive.

She had never seen it coming. She had never seen it as a possibility.

Would she give up everything for him?

No. She wouldn't. Because staying with him would mean giving up nothing.

He would be a partner. A lover. Her husband.

My husband is with me.

She thought of Freya, that goddess up in her heavenly plane, forever mourning the husband who was lost to her.

Fern had a husband. And he was not lost to her.

She needed to keep him. She needed to hold onto him.

She needed to have him. Forever.

Yes.

There was a whole world out there. Filled with many things. But in this room, with this man, she had found something that she hadn't even truly known existed.

She had found things out about herself. When she had been in that ballroom she had realized…her purpose was to help other people. It wasn't to go away and hoard her freedom, but to try to make life better for others.

For him, for their citizens.

She had been searching for a home all this time, and it was here. Not simply because it was a beautiful country, not simply because she wanted to help the people in it. But because of Ragnar.

It was his home. Branded on his soul. His blood was infused with it.

And she…she loved him. The totality of him. Which meant loving this place. Which meant being part of his mission.

He had been right all along. You couldn't outrun your destiny. What was meant for you could not be denied. Couldn't be turned away from.

They were what had always been meant to be.

A wave of desire rose up inside of her, and she wanted to fight against it because she was still breathless from her last orgasm, but she couldn't keep it from washing over her. She cried out his name.

She loved him.

It was a revelation.

It was glory.

Pain and pleasure and power and more than she had ever even dreamed of desiring.

She had imagined a life where she went off by herself and made all of her own decisions, but that was an illusion of freedom.

It was an illusion of happiness.

She hadn't been able to imagine caring about other people, thinking about other people, and being happy. Because living her life, living the way that she had in the palace in Cape Blanco, her family had made her miserable. And so she had imagined herself alone.

Oh, it was so much more work to care about another person. But she wanted to do that work. With him.

His face was set in stone as he continued to thrust inside of her, as he continued to chase his own release.

She could tell now that he was playing a game with himself. Prolonging it all. Holding himself back.

She smiled. She lifted her head and kissed his neck, kissed down to his collarbone. She felt his large body shudder, felt him pulse deep inside of her.

"Yes," she whispered into his ear. "Take me, Ragnar. I'm yours."

And that was when he let go.

His battle cry echoed off the walls as he surrendered to his need, as he spent himself deep inside of her.

And he gave himself over to the great and powerful need built up between them. And he pushed her over again. The unexpected force of her third climax making her cling to him so hard she was certain she drew blood.

He was breathing hard, and he moved away from her, lying on his back. He was breathing like he had been running. Like…

She looked at him; his eyes were glassy.

"Ragnar?"

She put her hand on his chest; she could feel his heart beating. "Are you okay?"

He growled, and gripped her around the wrist, flinging his body over the top of her again, but this time, it was as if he was shielding her.

"Ragnar," she said.

He rose up over her, looking somewhere back behind her, but there was nothing there but a wall. "Touch her and die."

She put her hands flat on his chest, held them there.

"Ragnar. No one is here. Nothing is happening. I swear to you. Nothing is happening."

And then, he made a terrible, strangled sound. Like that of a man being tortured. Physically, mentally.

Wherever he was, it was a dark place. Wherever he was, it might as well be hell.

"No."

He moved away from her then, his body shaking. He got off the bed, then he stood, like a man waiting to be taken to the executioner.

"Ragnar," she said again. "Please. Whatever is happening…"

And then it was like the fog had lifted. It was like he could see again. Like he was with her. He made a terrible sound. Like a wounded animal. One that had been gutted. And he fell to his knees, his head in his hands. "I remember," he said.

"Oh, Ragnar." She got out of bed and she went over to him. She knelt beside him, and she wrapped her arms around his shoulders. "What did you remember?"

He lifted his head, his blue eyes hunted, haunted. "It was my father. My father was the one that betrayed us all."

CHAPTER TWELVE

IT HAD BEEN like a thunderclap.

It had been nothing like he had ever expected. He hadn't thought much about regaining his past memories, not truly. Because he had always felt like it was a protection to him that he didn't remember. But he had thought that it was because it would be a terrible thing to remember the details of the deaths of his parents. Instead, it was the death of something else.

It was the death of every idea he had ever had about himself and his bloodline.

Yes, his father had been deemed somewhat selfish. A man who craved opulence. A man who loved the finer things in life, but he had never been accused of being a coward. A murderer. He had…

A sick, cold feeling slithered through his veins. As if his blood had turned to ice.

"He handed me over to a guard. To be killed."

"What?"

"He…he killed my mother. He killed her in front of me. He couldn't kill me."

"Ragnar. Slow down. Why…?"

"I think… I think he was working with them. I think he knew that they were going to take over, and the only way for him to save himself was to promise to leave and to never come back. But he also promised us. As…as some sort of sign that he… That he was sincere. That he was never going to reclaim his throne. He killed my mother. He killed her."

"No. He… That can't be right."

"It is," he said, knowing now exactly what had stolen his memory from him. Exactly.

Thankfully, his memory was that of a boy. He could remember hiding in the corner. His father raising a large knife. And he could remember his mother falling, her body obscured by the bed.

But it was unmistakable, what he had witnessed.

There were guards. Military men. "Take him. Dispose of him."

"It wasn't my nanny," he said, the realization rocking him to his core.

"What do you mean?"

"It wasn't my nanny who saved me. It was the soldier that my father gave me to. He took me away. He brought me to those people."

"Why did they tell you that it was a nanny?"

"I don't know. It must've been to protect him. It must've been. He must not have been able to kill a child. My father was too much of a coward to do it. He should've done it. He should have raised his sword and struck me down the way he did my mother."

"I still can't understand. Where is your father?"

"I don't know. For all I know they might have killed

him anyway, but he tried to get out of his own death in the most cowardly way possible. He betrayed us. He betrayed the country. He would see his own son killed."

"Oh…"

He put his hand on his forehead. Because then there were more memories. More and more.

His mother. Reading to him. It wasn't a nanny in his memory, telling him about Freya.

There is another way to be a warrior. One who leads with love.

"My mother," he said, his voice rough. "She was my best friend. She was the most important person in my life., I… My father, he was my hero. I saw him as a man who was strong. The kind of king that I wanted to be when I grew up.

"But my mother… She was the one who cared for me. She read to me every night. I felt so safe. I always felt so safe. The palace was my home, the seaside escape was a dream and I trusted them both."

"Of course you can't trust now. Of course everything feels like manipulation. Of course it all feels like a lie."

He looked at Fern, who looked devastated. Her green eyes were filled with tears, her complexion pale.

He had nothing to say to comfort her. Not when he felt entirely undone by the realization.

"It wasn't real. None of it. My father didn't love us. We were never the family that we appeared to be. Not if one day he could decide to raise his own hand against his wife." He pressed his hand to his stomach.

"I had no memories. I had filled those blank spaces with an idea, with an ideal. And none of it is true. My father was complicit in what happened to this country, to our family. He saved his own skin. But at the cost of everyone else. Everyone else. My mother, me, the citizens of Asland. Then he burned it so that no one would know he survived. I am… I am shot through with tainted blood."

"No," she said. "Don't say that. You aren't. You are brave. You are a man who has spent your entire life fighting against what happened to you. Because maybe you did tell yourself a new story. And maybe you didn't remember, but I believe that your body knew. And has known all this time. You are a good man. You brought yourself up from nothing to save this country, and your father never would've done that. He would've laid down and died in the dirt. A man so cowardly that he would kill his own wife, and give his son over to be killed… He would never do what you did."

"I don't know that," he said.

He felt like an imposter. Suddenly it all felt like a lie. He had been meant to come back and rule this country. And yes, he had known that he would be a different sort of ruler to his father, but in many ways he had felt like he was restoring the rightful blood-line, but his father had sold it away. He had sold them.

He had betrayed them, and left them. He had sacrificed everything for his own gain.

Yes, he had lost the throne, but he had… What he was out there living?

The very idea made him feel sick. That his own father was out there watching all of this, watching the return of his son, watching him discover that he had not succeeded. From the comfort of...whatever new existence he had fashioned for himself.

"I will find him," Ragnar said. "And I will have him killed."

"Ragnar. I understand that you want revenge. But the work that you're doing here in this country is so important. And revenge..."

She stopped.

"What? What is it that you have to say to me?"

"Nothing. You saw your father kill your mother. I'm not going to tell you to take the high road. I can't say what would benefit your soul, not today. Not knowing that he did that. Not knowing that he passed you off to a soldier to be killed."

She was still sitting with him, on the floor, as she had been that morning that she joined him after they'd first made love.

"Of course you don't like to be too comfortable. The only time you ever were it all turned out to be a lie."

She was stroking his face, and he couldn't bear it. He couldn't bear any tenderness with the vile memory still echoing in his head.

"Leave me," he said.

"No. I don't want to leave you. You've been dealing with all of this by yourself for all this time and—"

"You didn't ask for this," he said. "You were supposed to escape. Escape toxic families, and all of the other baggage that you grew up with, and here you have found that my family was worse than yours could ever be. It sounds as if your father is a sniveling coward. But one who would never ever get blood on his own hands. My father was dripping with it. I despise him. I... I am unclean. His blood is in my veins."

"I don't know what to say," she said. But she still didn't leave. She put her hands on his face. "I don't know what to say because this is monumentally fucked up. Because there is no guideline or handbook for how to help somebody through this, but I'm here. I'm here. I'm not going to leave you."

"You should."

She looked at him, her green eyes measured. "We have an agreement. I promised you that I would stay married to you for at least two years, and I will keep that promise, King Ragnar. I will stay your queen. Because you can trust me. You can trust that I will do what I said, that I'm everything I appeared to be. I'm not lying to you. And I would never, ever betray you. I swear it."

Her vows came from deep inside of her, and she understood them. They were nothing like the vows they had spoken to each other at the wedding, in a language that she didn't comprehend.

She was promising to stay with him and... He had no idea how he was going to feel in five minutes, let alone over the next two years.

At the moment everything felt degraded. Destroyed.

He had been inside of her, and everything had felt

good. For a moment, everything had felt so good it was like all of the walls inside of him had ceased to exist. And that was when the memories had come.

It was why he couldn't afford to be too comfortable.

It had been a warning.

And he had let himself down by letting everything fall away when he was with her.

He had no one to blame for all of this but himself.

The truth is the truth, whether you know it or not.

Yes. That was true. He couldn't deny it.

But he also couldn't reconcile the terrible burden of knowing these things either.

It made him want to drain the blood from his veins.

It made him want to claw into his own skull and remove part of his brain. The part that knew these things.

He wanted to go back to the way things were.

He wanted to go back to not knowing them.

Then go back.

You don't have to be open like this. You don't need her. You don't need anyone. And you sure as hell don't need these memories.

Yes. He needed to get a grip on himself. He needed to go back to when he didn't know.

He could rule the country that way.

He never had to think about this. He never had to acknowledge it. Yes, it would mean never finding his revenge, and there was something unsatisfying about that. But he would be a better king, a better man, if he didn't have to face the reality of this.

He would go back. He would go back. He just needed to erect the barriers around his soul again.

That was like a memory too. This act of building up a wall inside of himself. Around those thoughts. Around everything that had happened.

He had done this once before, and he would do it again. He never had to think about this again. Not ever.

He never had to think about it again.

He stood up. "I will sleep in the other room tonight."

"Please don't."

"I must. It is for the best. Tomorrow we will go home."

And with that, the conversation was over.

In that he was determined.

CHAPTER THIRTEEN

HE WAS COMPLETELY inaccessible to her now. Whatever had been building between them had shattered the night that his memories had returned. And she didn't know what to do. She didn't know how to reach him.

But he had shut the door so firmly it was impossible for her to even have a conversation with him.

It didn't make her inclined to go to his bed, and he hadn't asked. The one night she had woken up, her heart in her throat, she had gone in and peered into his chamber, and had seen him sleeping on the floor.

A prisoner of the past.

And yet he wouldn't even acknowledge it.

And this was where she decided to do something that she would never normally do.

She decided to call her brother.

Ricardo was the least awful of her brothers. The middle of them, and extraordinarily handsome. He was also very well-connected. A bona fide man-whore who slept with anything that moved, had extracted information from each and every one of his partners.

He was the most terrible gossip in all the world,

and all of that information tended to keep him in the lifestyle that he had become accustomed to.

He wasn't the least bit trustworthy.

Which was exactly why she wanted to talk to him.

"Hola," she said, speaking quickly to him in Spanish.

"Fernanda? I'm surprised to hear from you."

"Not that you bothered to check in with me."

"You become a whole queen. What a boon."

"I guess."

"Are you going to invite me to come and visit?"

"That depends. I don't know that I want state secrets to end up splashed all over the global news."

"You wound me," he said, but he didn't sound the least bit wounded.

"Well, I imagine that you'll recover. But I do have something to ask you."

"A favor? You haven't even spoken to me casually in ages."

"I was sequestered in a convent, not that any of you ever asked."

He sighed heavily. "I'm sorry. I find it best never to ask about what our father is up to. There are certain things I don't want to know, because I don't want it to be incumbent upon me to keep any secrets for him."

"That I can understand."

"What is it you need?" he said, sounding much softer.

"I need to know if there are any rumors out there about the former king of Asland."

"Oh," her brother said. "That is some ancient history."

"I know. It's not exactly the lifestyles of the rich and viral. Which I know is much more your specialty."

"That is true. But I know some people that I could ask. What exactly do you want to know?"

"I've just been made aware that there is some reason to believe that the king could still be alive."

"And what do you think will be accomplished if you do find him?"

"He should pay. For what he did," she said.

"I see. Well, I'll see what I can find out. You know all you need to do is drip honey into the right year and usually you can find a trail."

"I trust you."

"You probably shouldn't," he said.

"Maybe not. But…for what it's worth, we were both raised in a family with our father. So we've both suffered."

There was silence on the other end of the phone. "Yes. Though you suffered the most. You didn't have the freedom to leave. Not like we did."

"Well, our oldest brother certainly doesn't have the freedom to do whatever he wants."

"No. That is true."

"It's reserved for those of us who are expendable," Fern said.

"But you were never expendable, Fern. You were something different to him. An asset in a completely different way. And I would never say that it was better. I managed to disappear into the crowd. And there is something to be said for that."

"I've escaped now."

"Into an arranged marriage."

"There's nothing arranged about it," she said. "I… I want to stay with him. But I have to figure out how to help him. I have to figure out how to help fix this."

"I am not very good at giving advice. I'm certainly not anyone whose life should be admired. What I can say is that you cannot help someone who does not wish to be helped. You could deliver his father to him trussed up like a Christmas goose and if he did not want to accept the gift, he wouldn't. If he did not wish for that to heal him, it would not. Our father doesn't wish to be a good person, Fernanda. There is no amount of offering salvation to him that would make him take it, because he does not believe he needs it. If your husband does not believe he needs healing, then there is nothing that will ever make him accept it."

"Is that why you never come home? There's nothing you can do to fix any of it."

"Nothing. And so I go and I live my life. Out here in the world where there are no arbitrary rules like the ones our father made. You could do the same."

She would have thought of this as the brightest, shiniest apple only a few weeks earlier. Now, she wasn't so sure. Yes, a man like her father was somewhere beyond saving.

But it was different.

"The choice has to come into it somewhere, Ricardo, and I don't just mean the choice to be healed. Ragnar didn't choose this pain. And he had no one to help him through it. He has no idea how to handle it still. That doesn't make him bad. And it doesn't make him broken. It only means it might take a little bit of work."

"But as far as I know, you did not choose to do this work, my sister."

"No. I did. I am choosing this."

"You could also choose to meet me in the French Riviera."

"I appreciate the offer. But that isn't going to work for me."

Love was something she hadn't seen when she was growing up in the palace at Cape Blanco. What she had seen was her mother surrendering all of herself, her father imposing his will on everyone and her brothers becoming islands unto themselves in order to survive it.

She had never really thought about what love looked like. It wasn't manipulation. And it wasn't sitting down and letting another person suck everything out of you.

It wasn't passive. It wasn't malevolent.

Love, she thought, was expensive. It had a cost. It took work.

Sacrifice.

Because yes, she could cut ties with everyone and everything; she could go to the French Riviera with Ricardo. She could have lavish parties, and drink her troubles away. She could live alone. Or she could dig in and do the work here. Wasn't he worth it?

This man who had been betrayed.

This man who had gone through life with no one. Wasn't she worth it?

Wasn't she worth all this hard work?

She was beginning to understand that the most important things in life were hard. And freedom was making the choice to do the hard thing.

The thing that held weight. Had real value. Yes, she had dreams about a little farm. But that was just… It was a dream from an old version of herself. Who hadn't truly known everything that she was capable of. Who had thought that she could only hear herself, find herself in the quiet.

But she knew different now. She knew that she could stand strong, be the person that he needed and in turn the person that she needed.

"The next time we have a party, I'll call you."

"Thank you," he said. "In the meantime, I'll see what I can find."

And while she waited, she would have to decide what she was going to do about her husband.

Would she be like Freya? Waiting and waiting?

No. She was a goddess. And if she was a goddess, then she was going to go and make something happen.

It was late, and she wasn't quite certain where she might find him.

She had a feeling he wasn't in the palace, even if she couldn't say why. She put on a coat, and went outside into the harsh weather. The season was changing, and the harsh climate here was growing teeth.

So of course he would be out here. Of course he would be out here punishing himself.

Sleeping in the stable. As he had done when he was a boy.

She tore across the grounds, and went into the stable, where she saw him, standing by the stable with his horse.

His horse.

The horse meant something to him. Something important. He hadn't told her. He had come to get her on a horse, which was ridiculous.

"Why did you ride the horse to come and get me?"

He looked at her, his blue eyes shadowed.

"Please," she said. "Talk to me."

"For a number of years he was the only constant in my life. My most trusted…friend."

"See, you have had friends. Soren. Your horse. Me."

"We are not friends, Fernanda."

His use of her name hurt.

"You said that we were."

"Things have changed. I am reminded of who I need to be."

"Please, Ragnar. I don't want things to be like this between us."

"They cannot be another way. I cannot be a different man. I can't… I have to be the king."

There was such a weight to those words. Especially with what he knew now. He had to be the king.

He had to be beyond reproach. He couldn't have any weaknesses. Because now he was comparing himself to his father even if he didn't think he was.

"You are not your father."

"I don't wish to speak about that."

"It's important that you realize that."

"I have not spoken to you since we came back. Do you not realize that it was intentional? I am not asking for your advice on anything. I'm not asking for you to heal me."

Her brother's words echoed in her head.

"But maybe you should. Maybe you should ask for some help. Goddammit, Ragnar. Maybe you could be happy."

"Happiness has never been important to me. What is important is fulfilling my duty."

"And what about me?"

"You were never anything but a means to an end."

"Liar," she whispered. "I am Freya. And that means something, it matters. It means—"

"*Nothing*. Nothing but fractured memory in my fractured brain. It meant nothing."

He moved away from the stable, and stormed outside, into the wind. She followed. "I didn't take you for a coward."

"I am nothing like a coward," he said, the wind was blowing at his back, the cloak that he was wearing catching the breeze. And she could see that it was the one he had worn to their wedding. With the strip torn off.

"You made vows to me," she said. She pointed at his cloak. "You promised yourself to me."

"And I already told you. It is not binding, as it is not a promise I made to any deity that I believe in."

"And that's how life works for you, isn't it? You think that you can set your own reality with what you believe, and acknowledge and don't believe, and don't remember. But it isn't true. You don't get to decide. You don't get to decide what's real. You cannot fashion a new truth just to suit yourself. We made those vows. And I don't care if it's to a God you believe in. I believed what I said."

"You didn't," he said. "If I recall correctly you told me it was the most misogynistic thing that you had ever heard."

"Not those vows. The promise that I made to you that night in the hotel. I gave myself to you, and I meant it. And you don't get to control how I feel. You don't get to control what I want."

"I don't have to give you anything in return either."

He began to walk away and she reached out and grabbed the edge of his cloak. He stopped walking, even though she knew full well that he didn't have to. He gripped the edge of his cloak, and tugged it toward himself, bringing her along with it. And then he kissed her. Fern sensed the storm that was beginning to rage around them. She felt raindrops against her face, the wind picking up.

"Is this what you want?" He separated from her, his eyes wild.

"I want you," she said. "Real and raw and difficult. I want you."

"You may regret that."

His kiss was ferocious. Overwhelming. His lips bruised her, and she leaned in for more.

He was trying to frighten her, and she was trying to prove that she was strong enough to stay.

He needed to believe that there was poison in his veins. He needed to believe that something was broken irrevocably, because he was trying to protect himself. And now he was trying to prove that he was stronger than this thing between them, but she knew better.

She was stronger.

Because she had made her choice.

He gazed down at her, his blue eyes visible even in the darkness.

"My husband is far away from me," she said, touching his face. "And I miss him."

The growl that reverberated through his body was feral. Unlike anything she had ever heard. And that was when she found herself being laid down on the ground, cold and wet; he didn't care, and neither did she.

He tore at her dress, and she tore at his clothes, until his cock was free, until he thrust inside of her. There was no game being played. There was no tally being kept of who was satisfying who, and who had the upper hand.

It was a mutual claiming.

A mutual race toward either heaven or hell—which, it was difficult to divine.

He claimed her, over and over again, and she gave him back as good as he gave. Thrust for thrust. Until she cried out his name in time with the first rumble of thunder that rolled through the air.

And he clutched her hips and came, silent in defiance of the magnitude of it all.

"I love you," she whispered, touching his face. The rain poured down, droplets sliding through the creases by his eyes, nature shedding tears for him that he could not shed for himself.

"I love you," she said again. "I'm staying. I'm choosing to stay with you. It's not going to be two years. It's going to be forever."

He pulled away from her, snarling like a wounded beast. "No," he said.

"Yes," she responded. "You need me. You need me, and I need you. And I want to see this through."

"You need to leave, Fernanda."

He pulled away from her and stood up, and she clambered to her own feet, brushing at the wet spot on the back of her dress, shaking, trembling still from the aftermath of the pleasure that had been followed up by so much pain.

"That isn't how life works when you share it with another person, Ragnar. You are not my king. You are my husband."

"And it was only meant to be temporary."

"Bullshit. When you ran that horse across the Isle of Skye and stole me from the convent you didn't intend for any of this to be temporary. I asked for it to be, and now I have changed my mind."

"And I haven't changed mine. In fact, I aim to give you your choice, Fernanda. You will take my plane, and it will fly you anywhere in the world. Anywhere you wish to go. But you cannot stay here."

"What about your...your diplomacy?" she spat.

"I don't care about it. I don't care about this game. I don't care about anything except being the king I need to be, and I cannot do it with you here."

"You're scared. You are so afraid of your feelings."

"And maybe you would be too," he roared. "Maybe you would be too if the center of your feelings contained an image of your mother's dead body on the floor. A realization that your father is a monster. I knew love. And it betrayed me, brutally. I will never love again."

"Then I'm sorry for you," she said. "Because when I fell in love with you I found my strength for the first time. I could have left, Ragnar. At any time. And I could've decided to keep to our original agreement, but I have decided that loving, and living, and feeling all of this pain is worth something."

"If you ever have to look into the sightless, lifeless eyes of your own mother, then you can speak to me about pain. If you know what it is to grow up with nothing and no one, and more comfortable with the floor for a bed than a mattress, then you can speak to me of pain. You are a spoiled, selfish princess, Fernanda, and you not getting to go to whichever party you fancy, or marry whichever man you find hand-some, is not actually the struggle that you think it is."

A few weeks ago that would have hurt her. Maybe even shamed her. But she was not going to let this frightened fool of a man hurt her. She wasn't going to let him minimize what she had learned. What she knew now.

"I don't know the exact pain that you've gone through. But I know what it means to be lonely. I am sorry. I am so sorry that you were hurt the way that you were hurt, and I want to help you. And if you won't let me help you, just let me love you."

"Just like your mother? You would like to love me until your eyes grow dim? Until you lose every bit of yourself. Until you forget that you were ever a war-rior? Because you know that is what loving some-one broken brings. If it doesn't bring about your own death."

"You're not your father."

"No. And I can never afford to be. You...you make me weak. And I cannot afford it. The plane will leave in the morning. I've said my piece. This is done. It's over. You have your freedom."

"And what about my choices?"

"You are free to choose anything. Except me."

CHAPTER FOURTEEN

THE NEXT MORNING he watched the plane leave, watched as Fern left. He had demanded it. And she had obeyed. And yet, even as he got what he wanted, he felt as if his chest was being split open.

He was…destroyed in a way he hadn't thought possible.

He was ashamed of himself. Of the way that he had taken her last night. Of the way that he had taken a proclamation of love and thrown it back in her face, but he had no idea what else he was supposed to do with it.

Because it was far too terrifying. Far too powerful.

And so he had lied to her when he'd said that he couldn't feel fear. The moment that she had said she was going to stay with him…he had felt fear like he had never known before.

Deep, unending, primal fear.

But what did life look like without her? He could do this. He could continue to rule the country exactly as he had started. But now he…he knew.

Now he knew that there was something sweeter, something happier available for him if only he wanted it.

How ridiculous that he had thought that he could be with her for two years, and simply replace her with another wife.

He would never want another woman. Not as long as he lived. How would anyone ever be like Fern?

Freya.

His goddess.

There is another way to be a warrior...

His mother's voice echoed in his head, and he pushed it away.

Because it was far too painful.

It was far too...

It was a reminder of what love really is.

Of the fact that it didn't have to be defined by loss.

No. He refused.

He stormed around the castle, and found it far too comfortable for his liking. Every piece of furniture so soft and inviting. Everything inside of him was breaking apart. It took hours for him to be able to sit. For him to even contemplate eating.

And then his phone rang.

It was from a number he didn't recognize.

He answered. "Hello?"

"Hola. My name is Ricardo. You have just sent my sister to me."

"Fern."

"Yes. Fernanda is with me. She also tasked me with something. And even though I'm furious at you because my sister has come to me broken, she says that I still have to tell you this. I have found your father."

He felt like he had been hit in the chest with a brick. "Explain."

"I found your father. He's living in a small village in Spain. New name, new identity. Lots of money. I can have him brought to you."

"How?"

"I have my ways. But he can be taken captive, and brought to you if you like."

"Yes. I would very much like that."

He felt numb. His father was going to face justice.

And while nothing that happened would ever be made right, it would be… Something could be healed.

What about you?

There was something that still felt profoundly broken in him. And even as he prepared to receive the man that he hated more than any other, he felt no real triumph.

Because nothing in the past could truly be fixed.

And he had no idea what he wanted in his future.

It was world news. The former king of Asland had been found, living a secret life in Spain, and had been taken into custody. Imprisoned for crimes against his people, and also for murder.

She had been proud. Because he hadn't simply killed his father. He had allowed justice to prevail. He would now be sharing a cell with the other man who had destroyed the country.

It was fitting.

And she still felt devastated. Lonely.

She still missed him.

She still wanted him.

But she could be glad that some part of him had found... Perhaps justice would put him on a path to healing.

Perhaps it would placate something in him.

She was sitting by the pool at her brother's villa. She was more than one margarita into the day, and she was realizing that she needed to get herself together. She wasn't going to sit in her heavenly plane mourning a man who wouldn't come to her for the rest of her life.

She could at least be happy that this had given her a small chance to get to know Ricardo a little bit better. But she had also gotten to know his current boyfriend, and she liked him very much, and if Ricardo did his typical thing and blew it all up then she was going to be cross with him. She had told him that last night after dinner and he had only laughed.

"So I should attempt heartbreak like you?"

"You should not be an idiot like my husband. If you have a good thing you should keep it."

He hadn't been amused by that.

She took another sip of her margarita and looked out at the pool.

"You should slow down on those," said her brother, meandering near her lounge chair.

"Why? It's more fun than thinking."

"I agree. But you are much smarter than I am. You

also engineered justice that was long overdue. Not something I would've done."

"You did help."

"I did. Though I confess it was not initially out of the goodness of my heart. Just guilt."

"Some would suggest that your capacity for guilt means that you do have a good heart."

"I don't know about that."

"Vincenzo certainly seems to think you have a good heart."

"That's not what he likes."

"I disagree."

"Excuse me."

They both turned to see Vincenzo standing in the doorway. For a second, she was worried that he had overheard them.

"You seem to have a visitor," he said.

She and Ricardo exchanged glances. "I'm not expecting anyone," he said.

"I believe it's your sister's husband. I recognize him from all the recent news."

Her heart leaped up into her throat. She could scarcely believe it.

And then there he was, as if he had been summoned. Entirely incongruous in this sun-drenched setting, an ice-cold Viking, and her in a bikini.

She stood up slowly. "What are you doing here?"

"I'm here to thank you. And your brother. For what you have done not just for me but for my country."

Of course. He would be noble in the face of all of

this. She didn't want nobility. She didn't want a consolation prize.

What she wanted was him. But she needed that to be love. Not just desire.

"I did it for my sister," Ricardo said, colder than Ragnar at this point, which was impressive, honestly.

He gestured to Vincenzo, and the two of them went into the house. Leaving her and Ragnar alone.

"I contacted Ricardo about finding your father before I was sent away."

"Does that mean you wouldn't have done it?"

"I would have. It was the right thing to do. I knew that he would be able to help. He's very well-connected."

"I thought your whole family was worthless?"

"Not all of them. Something I'm discovering is that we were all raised by our father. And we have all made mistakes as a result of that. But not all of my brothers are proud of those mistakes."

"That is healing, I imagine."

"And what about you?" She looked at him directly. "Do you feel healed? Now that you know the truth?"

He shook his head slowly. "It was the right thing. But you know, a narcissist will always tell you that he did what he had to. He is incapable of being a villain in his own mind. There is nothing satisfying in talking to my father. He expressed pride that I lived. And in many ways I feel takes credit for it. There is no remorse. There is no satisfaction. It is only a tragedy, and we all must live in the aftermath. The only tragedy for him is that the end of his triumph is here. But there is no real...feeling."

"I'm sorry. I am sorry about all of it."

"Fern I... I need you to forgive me. There is so much about being human that I don't understand."

His words were soft, slow. It was all very unlike him. Her heart sped up, and then slowed down. "What do you mean?"

"You are right. I saw myself and you as symbols. And I began to make progress, but that progress felt too intense, and so I pulled away. That progress was what knocked the walls down inside of me and brought my memories back. It's why I ran from you. Why I turned away so resolutely. Because being with you made me feel safe for the first time in years. And that was what brought those memories out. I... I built a wall around them when I was a child. I didn't want to know that my father did that. I didn't want to remember what had happened to my mother. Or that he wanted me gone. It was easier. To survive. As long as I believed that the villain had come from outside of our family. I couldn't handle the truth."

"Few people could. It's a monstrous thing to have to face. It's... Few people could've survived what you did. You did what you had to do."

"Yes, I did. But somewhere along the line, I was okay. I just didn't feel like I was. I forgot that I was doing more than surviving. It's the only thing I know how to do. I do not know how to live, Fern. Except... I kept remembering that my mother is the one that told me the story about Freya."

"And what did she tell you?"

"The reason that some warriors don't go to Valhalla is because they choose a different path. They fight for love and not glory. They fight for love most of all, above honor, above country. She cared about that. It was what she wanted me to know. Because I think…my father wanted his own glory. He spoke of Valhalla. My mother… She wanted me to love. And all of these years took that away from me. That understanding. That story. You brought it back."

"I did?"

"Yes. You did."

"I still love you, you know," she said. "It didn't go away just because you weren't ready."

"Oh, Fern." He moved forward and touched her face. "I am grateful for that. I am so much more than grateful. Because I want to change. I want to learn to live. But I'm going to need you to do it. I… I think I love you. For all that it's worth, coming from a man who has spent his life building walls around his heart."

She moved forward, and gripped his hand. "That means even more."

It was like their wedding, except there was no cloth binding their hands together. It was only them. Only their choice. Only their love.

"Would you come with me?" he said. "Please."

"Yes," she said.

He took her hand, and led her through the house. Her brother and Vincenzo were sitting on a chaise, and watched as they went past.

"I'm going with him," she said. "Thank you," she said. "For everything."

"I expect an invitation to a party," Ricardo said. "And," he added, "if you break my sister's heart, King Ragnar, there is no corner of this earth that will be able to conceal you. Remember, I found your father."

"I'm not my father," Ragnar said. "I stand and fight my battles."

"Even if you're a little late," Ricardo pointed out.

And Ragnar surprised her by laughing. Really laughing. Perhaps the first real laugh she had ever heard from the man. "Yes," he agreed. "I was a little late indeed."

He opened the front door for her, and for a moment she thought she was hallucinating. Because there was a horse. His horse, in fact, right outside.

"You brought your horse?"

"Yes. I bring him to every important battle. I would never trust myself if I left him behind."

"Are you superstitious?"

"Yes. I told you. I believe in trolls and giants. And luck."

He mounted his horse, and extended his hand. She accepted, and he pulled her up onto the steed, nestled right at his front. It was so very different to that first time. Where he had run her down in the field. This time, she was going very much willingly.

"I also believe in Freya," he whispered against her ear. "And I worship at her altar. And will, for the rest of my life."

He didn't need to say it. She knew that it was true. He was driven by love. Whether he knew it or not, he always had been. The love for his people, the love for a mother that he had lost.

And now, his love for her. He had never been a man who felt too little. Only a man who felt too much.

But now all that feeling had somewhere to go.

Now, he wasn't alone anymore.

She looked back at him, into those brilliant blue eyes.

Blue, as far she could see. Wild, untamed.

And in his eyes, she saw the future. Their future. Their love, their marriage, their children.

Forever.

And in his arms, she finally felt like herself.

Fern.

His chosen queen, who had absolutely chosen him back.

* * * * *

If you couldn't put From Convent to Queen *down, then be sure to check out these other desire-fueled stories from Millie Adams!*

His Highness's Diamond Decree
After-Hours Heir
Dragos's Broken Vows
Promoted to Boss's Wife
Heir of Scandal

Available now!

Get up to 4 Free Books!

We'll send you 2 free books from each series you try PLUS a free Mystery Gift.

FREE Value Over $25

Both the **Harlequin Presents** and **Harlequin Medical Romance** series feature exciting stories of passion and drama.